NOT ALONE
The birth that changed the world

Charles G. Dorsey

PRAIRIE MUSE BOOKS INC

2020

This is a work of fiction. Names, characters, places, and incidents
either are the product of the author's imagination or are used fictitiously.

NOT ALONE
Copyright © 2020 by Charles G. Dorsey
Paperback Edition
ISBN: 978-1-952911-11-8

Prairie Muse Publishing
Lincoln, Nebraska 68520

FOREWORD

I grew up in a small town in northeastern Iowa in a Christian home and from the time I learned to read, had a book in my hand. Now many years later, I am still reading two to three books a week. The one book which has always been special to me above all others is the Bible.

Even though I have read many books about the Bible, I always go back to the Bible itself. There is no other book like it. In this book, I have found history, geography, government, family, occupations, personal tragedies, wars, personal failures, successes, and above all love and faithfulness of the creator God.

The stories from the Bible have always held a particular fascination for me and I have wondered and dreamed about the people who were living at the time of its stories, and were around to see the things we are told about in the Bible.

This book is fiction, but I have tried to put as much into these sketches as I can. I also hope you will become curious to learn even more as I have designed questions into this work. Jesus was a real person, as were those living around Him at the time He walked on this earth.

This is just a short writing of many of the thoughts I have had over the years. I hope you enjoy and learn as you read this. I have tried to be diligent to not add, subtract, or alter the Bible in any way.

Chuck Dorsey

ACKNOWLEDGEMENTS

Thank you to my wife, Mary, for the love and patience she has shown through this process. Although the book is short, the time to write it in the proper manner took much longer than I had hoped. She also put up with my books everywhere. She also gave huge input, just talking with me that she was not even aware of. She is not only part of my heart but a terrific contributing partner to my thinking about the Bible. Only with her help have I been able to finish.

Besides my wife, there are three pastors I have received input from and they most likely do not know how much they have helped me in this endeavor. These three are Joel Harmon, Mark Brunott, and Nat Crawford. All have contributed to my spiritual wellbeing and have encouraged me on the way.

Thank you Joel, Mark, and Nat.

PREFACE

It has always been my belief that we are never truly alone, even during those times when we feel the absence of anyone else so greatly. We are seen, we are heard, we are felt, and we can even carry on a conversation while feeling lonely.

What we forget is that many times everything we say, do, or feel is heard, seen or felt by someone else. Even more important is that everything we are experiencing during these times affects some other person in some way, although many times that effect is exceedingly small. And even though we may never know it, the resulting effect can be of extreme, long-lasting importance.

So it was in the tiny village of Bethlehem some 2000 years ago. An unknown couple in an obscure part of what was then known as the Roman Empire, quietly appeared in the small town of Bethlehem in the dim evening light and found lodging only in the stable of the inn.

Here they gave birth to a baby boy who became the focal point of man, angels, and all of history from that time forth. This baby brought with him—and actually was—the promise of the future for the entire world.

But not all of the people who were around this tiny baby that night were affected in the same way. These short personal sketches are of some of those people who may have been there the night Jesus the Christ was born or shortly after his birth.

Not all of these people knew or cared what had happened. Some were excited, some were offended, others did not care, but all were or would be affected.

It is about some of these people who may have been there that is the point of these sketches.

Part 1

A small town called Nazareth in the northern part of Israel

The Night of the Beginning

It was just another night in the ancient land of the Hebrews. It was springtime. The crops had been harvested and there was now time for a short break from the field work. It was also a special time of giving thanks for the bounty with which Jehovah, God, had blessed His people.

This was a country that had seen many generations of families and kingdoms. There had been countless battles and disputes with other nations over control and protection of many different kingdoms, depending on who was the ruling government at the time. Woven in also were times of peace.

The stories of kings, good and bad, were remembered in stories handed down by the fathers and grandfathers to the next generation. These stories were stored and maintained in the memories of every person. This was the way the Hebrews kept their identity as a nation through the many generations from the beginnings of the country by the twelve sons of Jacob, whose name was changed to Israel by Jehovah.

The Hebrew nation actually started while in slavery in Egypt, hundreds of years earlier.

This land of Israel was located at the east end of the Mediterranean Sea and in the middle of most of the history that had marched across the known world. Many of the trade routes that had been developed between the east and west crossed through this area of land once known as Canaan. Caravans made up of camels and asses made the long treks across the hot deserts on the east and the west, and the sparse river valleys. Trade was strong and active because it was the only way to obtain silks and fragrances from the Eastern parts of the world, and other goods from the west. Many goods from the East such as silks and spices were desirable to those who could afford to pay for them. Because of this trade, strange and different languages were a common part of life for the people who lived along caravan routes.

Israel was at the central part of the known world through much of history, and the land was coveted because of its location. The Roman government ruled most of the known world and wanted all the rest. Israel, with the caravan routes coming through there, was especially important to the power of Rome. The Romans had grown to be the most powerful government known, and ruled with an iron hand and a sharp sword. To them, there was room for no one else to govern and no one else was tolerated.

Palestine, the name the Romans gave to Israel when they gained control of this area, was a land of many rocks, little water except in the valleys and the few wells, and best suited for flocks of sheep and goats, animals which survived on seasonal grazing.

The inhabitants of Israel had adapted to the soil and the climate, and outside of the periods of time when the battles over domination of the land were raging, it was an area of very close tribes and families with a particular separation from foreign countries and peoples. The people of Israel believed they had been chosen by the supreme being, known to them as Jehovah, creator of the world, to be a holy people, separate from all other peoples. They also believed that Jehovah had given this land to them and them alone. No matter how much or how many times they were displaced, they would again somehow return.

Over the land, Roman soldiers patrolled either in groups or individually, going about their duties. Many times their duties did allow personal time when everything was quiet.

The soldiers lived a strange dichotomy—that of when being in rank or formation, showing forth a perfectly organized total power, but when not on a duty or a mission, giving the real person inside the uniform a chance to relate to other people, even the people over whom they ruled, in a personal way.

While the soldiers were in ranks, any civilians walking or in the way were often nudged, pushed, or even kicked to make way for the military. At the same time, many of the soldiers off duty were extremely personable and in their private lives gave a totally opposite impression from the military harshness. However, the rule over the people was an absolute rule, no questions asked, no exceptions tolerated.

The Roman government managed its many different peoples in an unusually open way, giving them freedom to lightly govern themselves but requiring two main things. They could make no rules or laws that contradicted Roman law, and taxes must be paid completely and on time. The Romans maintained the total right to decide how high the taxes were to be, and could and would at any time raise them. Taxes could also be collected at any time chosen by the Roman Empire rulers.

The night this started, all seemed to be quiet in the land of Israel. Sheep in the fields or in their folds were quiet, most lying down for the night, resting secure in the presence of their shepherds. The partial moon was high, and with the stars in the sky, was lending its gentle glow to the hilly, rocky landscape. Only the sounds of the nocturnal animals disturbed the quiet, looked down upon by the silent and restful sky. Families were also in their homes asleep on their mats. It was just another quiet night, except...

In one of the dwellings of the town known as Nazareth, in the northern part of the land of Israel, in a corner given to a young maiden, an eerie light suddenly appeared, waking the girl from her sleep. It was very bright, but at the same time soft and gentle as a caress. It was a light of indescribable beauty and seemed to illuminate everywhere and yet did not reach or even touch the others sleeping in the house. It rested on and surrounded the young girl for a short while and then, just as suddenly as it came, it was gone, leaving again only the light from the night sky glowing through the open window on her corner of the room.

The young maiden was now again alone, but standing quietly in the dark, thinking about what she had just experienced and heard, and looking out of the window at the peaceful night sky.

When she finally lay down on her mat, sleep did not come

easily, if at all. Her mind was totally inundated with the night visit of the being who could only be described as an angel coming from heaven.

The message she had been given by the angel was so bizarre she had accepted it as truth. There was no other way to understand it. Somehow, her entire being was overwhelmed by the words of the angel.

As sleep slowly came, so did the questions. What does this all mean? What should she do now? How should she tell her parents? What about her betrothed? She had never been with a man, but was going to have a baby.

She unconsciously touched her abdomen as she again and again rehearsed the words the angel, as she now had accepted who her visitor had been, had spoken to her. Why had the Supreme Holy God chosen her?

THE STORY FROM THE BOOK OF LUKE

LUKE CHAPTER 1, VERSES 26 THROUGH 38 (ESV)

In the sixth month, the angel Gabriel was sent from God to a city of Galilee named Nazareth, to a virgin betrothed to a man whose name was Joseph, of the house of David. And the virgin's name was Mary. And he came to her and said, "Greetings, O favored one, the Lord is with you!" But she was greatly troubled at the saying, and tried to discern what sort of greeting this might be. And the Angel said to her, "Do not be afraid, Mary, for you have found favor with God. And behold, you will conceive in your womb and bear a son, and you shall call his name Jesus. He will be great and will be called the Son of the Most High. And the Lord God will give to him the Throne of his father David, and he will reign over the house of Jacob forever, and of his kingdom there will be no end."

And Mary said to the angel, "How will this be, since I am a virgin?"

And the angel answered her, "The Holy Spirit will come upon you, and the power of the Most High will overshadow you; therefore the child to be born will be called holy—the Son of God.

"And behold, your relative Elizabeth in her old age has also conceived a son, and this is the sixth month with her who was called barren. For nothing will be impossible with God."

And Mary said, "Behold, I am the servant of the Lord; let it be to me according to your word." And the angel departed from her.

A Mother in Israel

In the very same household the morning came just as it did on any normal day in Israel. The family was up and the morning meal completed. The father had gone to his work, and the younger children were playing gleefully outside of the house with whatever they could find or dream up. The oldest of the girls was helping her mother with the morning chores and preparations for the day's food. After the house duties were completed, the children would be back inside for their lessons.

Lessons were taught from the memory of the mother, and the young children were trained to commit all things to memory. There were no books or scrolls in the individual homes. Those were kept in the local synagogue and were read on the Sabbath by the Rabbi or the leaders of the community. They were also used by the local Rabbi for teaching the boys during school hours. The boys were sent to the Rabbi's school when they reached a certain age while the girls remained under the instruction of the mother.

Lessons for both boys and girls included the history of the Jewish people, especially the law as given by Moses, music from the Psalms, and for the girls of course, cooking for a family, as that would be the primary responsibility of a woman of that time.

These teachings stored in their memories were often spoken of and confirmed regularly by the men while at work, and by the morning gatherings of the women at the well while drawing water for the home. Things they had learned from their husbands were also discussed and confirmed and solidified into consistent and regularly accessible memories. This was the primary mode of education for this unique people chosen by God Himself to carry a promise of the future—a promise they were to keep in their hearts—looking forward with great daily anticipation to the coming of the promise, "The Messiah", and never to cease speaking of it.

Since most girls knew early who they were to spend their life with in marriage, they were taught home duties focusing on being a quality wife as well as a future mother of multiple children as God chose to bless them. A boy first, they hoped, but girls also. Besides the home, the girls spent much time memorizing the old scriptures, learning about the history of their people, and every detail known about the fathers of their tribes and the father of their nation himself, Abraham, the father of all nations to be.

To help the people's memories, there were feasts and gatherings to be celebrated at regular times of the year. Also, there were sacrifices to be offered to God at proper times and places. All of these were for the purpose of reminding the people who they were and who Jehovah, God, wanted them to be.

All this was important, especially for the young girls, for in some cases the ages of marriage partners was quite disparate.

The mortality rate was very high, and many times a very young woman would be married to an older man who already had children. The training of the children was the mainstay of the nation, and the young bride needed to be prepared to care for a home and nurture children of all ages.

But that was not the case for the daughter of this household. The father of this house had made a contract of marriage with the father of a young single man who was not only the son of a good friend but had been well trained in the art of carpentry, an extremely honorable occupation. This young man was a man whose work was reputed to be some of the best in the area. The two young people were now in the one-year engagement period that the custom stated was required before the marriage ceremony. This period was a special time for her to focus on becoming a wife. In many cases, the two to be married had known each other since childhood.

The mother was extremely proud of her daughter who was thought of as the example for all the other maidens of the town to follow. Mary's attitude and service to her family and to others of the community was above reproach and often spoken of by the other women.

So on this particular morning when Mary came to her mother to share something special she had experienced during the night, the mother focused her attention on her soon-to-be-married daughter. Her daughter seemed unusually agitated this morning, sort of excited but unusually pensive; joyful, but at the same time a quietness seemed to surround her. The young girl looked directly at her mother and began her story.

As the mother listened, her whole being went into a state of total amazement. Her daughter had often dreamed about her life as a married woman, but this was something totally new and unexpected. She struggled to grasp what she was hearing.

Her daughter was describing a visitation from a heavenly being—one who not only gave his name, but claimed to stand in the presence of Jehovah, Himself, and had come with a message especially for her. Moreover, this messenger had told her that she was favored by Jehovah and would become pregnant and bear a son who would rule all of Israel.

While the mother was trying to take all this in, the daughter also told her mother that she had agreed to do what the messenger from God had asked. She would serve Jehovah.

For a while, after the daughter left to do errands, the mother just sat in one place trying to comprehend all her daughter had had been told. She would have a son. His name was to be Jesus. He will be great. He will be called the "Son of the Most High." He will be given the "Throne of David". He will reign over the "House of Jacob" forever. His kingdom would have no end.

The mother thought about what she had heard and tried to make some kind of sense of what had happened. Was her daughter dreaming, or overwrought about the marriage? How should she tell her husband? What about her daughter's betrothed? What would he think?

The mother sat quietly thinking about all the different things this could and would affect if it were to take place. She thought about how she would tell her husband. This was not something she could or should easily share with the ladies at the well. And what if it were true? How could she survive the attitudes of the community and the others who had lived close to them for so long? How would they interpret the story she had to tell?

The mother sat quietly meditating for a very long time. Finally, with her mind spinning, she arose and began going about her daily duties of teaching the children and maintaining the household. Then she remembered another message she had just received. This was about her aging cousin Elizabeth. Elizabeth was well past the childbearing age but was now pregnant. This was not normal. Was there a heavenly visitor involved there also? Were the two connected? Perhaps a visit by her daughter to this cousin would help explain this whole thing. Her cousin's husband was a well-respected priest. Perhaps there could be some answers. Her daughter could be of help to this aging cousin and her husband, especially with the pregnancy in the latter stages.

She also knew of a friend who would be traveling to the very area where her cousin lived, and Mary would be able to safely travel with them.

She called her daughter when she returned from her errands and asked her to prepare for a trip to visit her cousin. Perhaps this visit would give some explanation and understanding.

While her daughter was gone, she would find a way to talk to her husband who was a very proud man. Then she would make a plan.

Father of a Virgin

Joachim thought back upon all that had happened over the time since he had begun his relationship with his good friend, Jacob. They had been friends together as children and had maintained their friendship during the years of growing up, becoming men and even marrying. They had still been close when children came and it was only natural to decide that their children would join the two families together.

One of Jacob's sons, Joseph, had especially caught his attention. He had watched as his friend had trained this son, Joseph, in the skill of carpentry and had seen the high quality of his work. It showed excellence, far above the work one would expect from a young man of his age. His work was in demand from many of the small towns close by and was even spoken of in larger towns farther away. The love of his work was evident in the finished products he produced.

Joachim had also watched Joseph grow in wisdom as he

became a young man and grew to earn the respect of the entire town. He had early realized this boy would someday make an excellent husband and father. It was with this in mind that he had approached his longtime friend and asked if he would consider a contract for future marriage between the two.

His friend, Jacob, had also in turn been watching Mary, and a contract was early and properly arranged between the fathers. The two children were told of the contract from that date, and they had grown to know and understand each other, even talking of the day when they would be joined together as man and wife. Both families were pleased.

The proper time had come to announce the engagement, and with joy he had looked forward to the wedding and the future family growing with grandchildren. But then, without any warning, his wife had come to him and said, "We need to talk, for your daughter is with child."

It was like a knife in the heart. His daughter was considered to be the favorite of the maidens in the town. How could this happen? Why had this happened? He had all his life tried to live by the law that had come from Jehovah and guide his children in the same way. His daughter had never given a hint of stepping away from the pathway of the right. Of all the young maidens, why her? How could this be happening to his family?

It was his duty to tell the young man that his promised bride had been unfaithful. But how could he even begin to explain? And the story of the visit. An angel? Holy Spirit? What are these things?

There was also the matter of the law. She could be stoned! The family would be disgraced! Close as brothers for years, the father would not be able to lift his face to his future son-in-law, or his longtime trusted friend, or anyone else in the town.

To understand that his daughter had been unfaithful to her betrothed was more than he could comprehend. What words could he use to inform the young man that the agreement made so long ago had now been broken and all the dreams and plans had been shattered and were no more?

And what would Joseph do? The law was very precise in the rules for adultery, and even though they were not as yet officially married, they were considered by the engagement as married and the rules applied to them as if they were. That meant that even stoning could be a possible outcome for the breaking of the relationship.

He had grown quite close to Joseph and already loved him as his own son. How could Joachim cause him this great hurt? How could he break the heart of a person who had already become like one of the family?

And then there was his own daughter. He and his wife had done all they could to teach her the right way of life and she had grown in a way of thoughtfulness and consideration for others that was noticed by the whole town. His wife had seen to her skills as a homemaker and future mother. To be in this situation was just not right.

He had waited as long as he could, hoping that somehow his wife would turn out to be wrong and some other reason could be found to explain this. In the meantime, Mary had gone to the hill country to visit an aging cousin who had become pregnant at a very old age, (another strange event to ponder), but when Mary had returned, the evidence in her body was confirmation.

He had made his way slowly to the house of Joseph, his heart so heavy, it was difficult to even walk.

Now, in silence, he sat on the wooden bench just inside his own home, below the window, the soft moonlight finding him and sending sparkles from the drops of moisture in his beard—moisture that came from the tears flowing like little rivulets from his reddened and swollen eyes. It was even now into the third watch of night and he had been here since afternoon when he had returned from the house of Joseph. He had eaten no food and had spoken to no one but had gone to this bench in a state of self-searching, looking in vain for an answer. What could he have done wrong?

Again and again the tears seemed to find new reservoirs and began to wind their way down the sides of his cheeks, joining the tears already there in the despondent display of his heart.

Every word he had spoken to Joseph was burned into his memory.

Joseph, my son. You know that Mary has had only you in her eyes and heart, and has looked forward to the day when you would be joined in marriage. Today I have come to you with heavy heart to beg for your forgiveness, for I must tell you that Mary is with child. When I asked her how this could be, she told me that she had never known a man and has kept herself for you only.

Then she told us of a visit from a heavenly being who came to her one evening and revealed to her that she had been chosen to bear a son by the Holy Spirit, a child who would be called the "SON OF THE HIGHEST." This is beyond my understanding. If you know anything about this, please tell me for this is more than I can bear.

He remembered the look on the young man's face as he

received this news. It moved from shock, to horror, and then to unbelief, all of which showed in visible waves. He watched as Joseph worked to gain control of his emotions. There was a time of silence as both men thought about the event which had brought them to this place.

Then came the reply, spoken in the manner for which Joseph had become noted. *"I must think on these things. Tomorrow we will find an answer."*

They embraced and Joachim had left to make his way home the longest way possible. But the walking and time of reflection did nothing to lift the weight of pain on his heart. His body felt as though it had been torn apart by wild beasts. His head felt like the whole world was sitting on top of it. He begged and pleaded with Jehovah, but no answer came, only more tears to replace the ones slowly dried by the night air. He had not moved from this place the entire evening. The silence, the sadness, and the tears just continued.

Then the quietness of the night was broken by the sound of hastened footsteps coming toward the house. They grew louder and stopped at his very door and he heard the call of "Father, Father, Father!"

It was the voice of Joseph. He arose and hurried toward the door. But why would he come now? At this hour? What news could not wait till the morning?

THE STORY FROM THE BOOK OF MATTHEW
MATTHEW CHAPTER 1, VERSES 18 THROUGH 25 (ESV)

Now the birth of Jesus Christ took place in this way.
When his mother, Mary, had been betrothed to Joseph,
before they came together, she was found to be with child
from the Holy Spirit. And her husband, Joseph, being a
just man and unwilling to put her to shame, resolved to
divorce her quietly.

But as he considered these things, behold, an angel of the
Lord appeared to him in a dream saying, "Joseph, son
of David, do not fear to take Mary as your wife, for that
which is conceived in her is from the Holy Spirit. She will
bear a son, and you shall call his name Jesus for he will
save his people from their sins."

All this took place to fulfill what the Lord had spoken by
the prophet; "Behold, the virgin shall conceive and bear
a son, and they shall call his name Immanuel!" (Which
means, God with us)

When Joseph awoke from sleep, he did as the angel of the
Lord commanded him: He took his wife, but knew her
not until she had given birth to a son. And he called his
name Jesus.

Part 2

Bethlehem ◆ A town in Judea

The Tax Collector

Matthew, the young tax collector, sat in his booth just outside the small town of Bethlehem, watching for any stragglers who might still come late in the day. The booth was unbearably hot as the afternoon sun had moved slowly past the shade of the small skin roof which was his only meager protection during the high sun heat of the day. Most of the travelers relocating because of the census were already past and making ready for the evening meal. As he waited, looking down the road, his mind wandered back over the events which had caused him to be here in this place as a publican, a tax collector working for the Roman government.

Just two years ago Matthew had celebrated his thirteenth birthday and his bar mitzvah, his coming of age. He was now expected to act and carry the responsibilities of an adult. That meant he was to act like, talk like, and carry the workload as an adult. Then, shortly afterward, his parents had both suddenly become ill and died. As there were no close relatives and he was of age, Matthew was left to fend for himself. He had now become an orphan with no means of income and only an empty house to live in. He could not understand why Jehovah had allowed this to happen to him and for almost a year had worked at anything he could find available.

Then one day he had overheard a Roman soldier talking to a townsman, trying to convince him to work as a tax collector for the Roman government. Every person or town—large or small—was required to pay taxes, and someone had to do the work of giving an accounting of the amounts paid. There was also normally a booth at the edge of each town where travelers would pay a small or large tax on passage through or by the town. The size of the town often determined how much tax was assessed as also did the size of the load carried.

Bethlehem was small and known as a shepherd's town, so those that wanted to earn a lot of money did not want to practice their occupation here. The added stigma of collecting taxes for the ruling Romans meant someone accepting that position would be looked down upon by his friends and neighbors.

Following the Roman soldier, Matthew watched him asking several others in town without success. Waiting until the soldier was about to leave for the day, Matthew ran to the road to stop him, asking for the position and explaining that he was indeed of proper age, and as this town was small, it was worth taking a chance on him, even if he was young. Besides, he knew everyone here and was accepted by the people of the town. After all, if it didn't work out, he could come back and change it. The soldier had orders to find someone and decided he would take a chance on this young man.

Matthew had been smart enough to realize that he didn't have to charge a lot over the proper tax rate to make a profit; and because he had not charged exorbitant fees, he had at least been allowed by the residents of that area to make his collections without too much malice. That had been over a year ago and he now owned two houses—the one he had been left by his parents and one he had just purchased to help a family who needed finances to travel for the census.

He looked down at the pouch where he kept the money he had taken in that day. With so many people on the move to their ancestral city for the Roman census, it seemed his portion from the taxes had multiplied many times over. Bethlehem, here on the road to the center of trade in Jerusalem, was especially lucrative, even though very small.

He turned his attention down the road where he could see only two people moving in his direction. Whoever it was, they were moving very slowly.

This town of Bethlehem was the birthplace of King David, the most famous king in Hebrew history, and everyone wanted to be numbered as part of the lineage of the family of David.

Bethlehem was also listed in the prophesies as the birthplace of the Messiah, a descendent of David, and everyone wanted to be counted as family with the future "KING OF ALL", promised for many generations.

Well, Matthew had learned of the Messiah as a child like everyone else, but he had never seen a sign to indicate who he was or when he was going to come, especially now.

The Romans had an iron hand around everyone's neck, and if the Messiah did come, he would have a very heavy battle ahead of him in order to break Israel free of Roman domination.

Again he looked down the road. This time he could make out the moving figures. There were two together, and it turned out to be a man leading a heavily loaded animal; and it looked also like a woman was riding. She must be ill. Women did not normally ride but walked alongside their husbands. The beast was almost always used to carry the needs of the family, and sometimes children, should they be very young or tired.

As they came closer, Matthew could see that the woman was indeed surrounded by personal things but also by tools of a carpenter's trade.

He sat waiting silently as they moved toward the booth. The woman, he saw, was pregnant. The young man leading the animal approached the booth, not even trying to dodge the tax as many would do and asked directions to the inn.

Matthew told him where the inn was located and then added that he did not think there would be room there, because there were so many travelers for the census and also because it was so late in the day the inn would surely be filled.

The young man looked at his wife, then back to Matthew and said, "There must be room, for the baby will come tonight."

He then inquired the amount of the tax.

Matthew answered quickly, "Go and find room, I have no need of your money."

The young man looked at the tax collector strangely for a moment, and then said, "Shalom to you and your house."

He turned the beast carefully and moved away into the streets of Bethlehem. Matthew watched them slowly go until they turned a corner and moved out of sight, and then puzzled, thought over what had just happened, and his own response. *This man greeted me as if I were an acquaintance and not like some outcast animal as most of society did.*

In Israel, a tax collector was the lowest form of life because it was felt that they had sold out to the Romans. It was also common knowledge that a tax collector would charge as much as they could get out of the people in order to increase their profit. Even though he had not followed that line to the extremes that other tax collectors normally did, Matthew did overcharge the rich.

They could afford it.

But he also tried to be very careful of the poor. Even so, to society he was still a "Tax Collector," a "Publican."

At this, another startling thought came to his mind. *Why had he not collected the tax? He had never allowed that to happen before. No one passed without paying something. Why had he allowed them to pass? What was there about this man and woman that had caused him to act this way? He would like to meet and talk with them again. But how could he do that?*

He thought for a moment. *Wait! The man was a carpenter, and there were none in Bethlehem as they had all gone for the census. Many people needed work done as did he himself. Perhaps he would talk to his friend the innkeeper in the morning and inquire as to this couple. In fact, the one house that he had just purchased was not being lived in at the moment as it was being repaired. Perhaps he could convince them to live there. They needed a place to stay and he needed someone to rent his house, and the man could do the repairs.*

It would be good for everyone and best of all, he would be able to again talk to this couple who had such an effect on him.

Even though he was young, he had also learned to be very perceptive in his judgement of people. He just wanted to know more about this family.

With this plan conceived, Matthew took up his bag of money and turned toward his home.

The Innkeeper

This had been the busiest week of his life with people coming and going from seemingly everywhere. There were many former countrymen—now living in neighboring lands—passing through and stopping on their way to be counted for the census. He had heard languages he had never heard before and had seen forms of dress he had never imagined.

It was as if the whole world had just been put into a great mixing bowl and gotten stirred up, but of course the ruling Romans didn't care, as long as they got the numbers they wanted and the taxes they thought they needed. What was happening to people, even families, meant nothing to them. Actually, as long as taxes were paid regularly and no Roman laws were broken, they left you alone.

He had seen many people come and go, this old innkeeper of Bethlehem. His father had owned the inn before him, and his father before that. Just as the memories of the old traditions were passed down, so were the occupations of families. His

son had an inn in a small town not far away. It would probably never change, the way of this people; it seemed like it had
always been and would always be. Just like waiting for the
Messiah, some ways just keep going on forever.

He thought of the morning meal with his young friend,
Matthew, the tax collector. They had talked just a few weeks
ago about Matthew's purchase of another house. It had been
more of a gift to the previous owners as they were without the
funds needed for the trip to the city of their ancestors, and
Matthew had also agreed to sell it back to the family after they
returned, if they did return.

So many of those going to another location just did not come
back. This census was not a short stay situation. It could easily
take several years before all the records the Romans wanted
would be finished. It was unusual for one so young to own so
much, but Matthew had listened carefully and followed the
innkeeper's advice and done well with his money. The morning meal shared often by the two of them had developed into a
mentorship-friendship relationship between the two.

The innkeeper had taken Matthew under his wing after
young Matthew had lost both of his parents suddenly to an
illness. He had helped the boy by giving him work and fed him
when he was running low on food.

He was shocked when Matthew told him of his appoint-
ment as a tax collector, a publican. He had warned the young
man of everything that he could think of about the prevailing
attitudes the people he had known and lived near all his life
would have about his new work.

Nothing he said could change the mind of his young

friend, and the innkeeper had then turned his mind to helping Matthew balance his chosen occupation with integrity
and consideration for other people.

Being a businessman himself, he had counseled Matthew
on how much to charge, when he could charge extra, and
when he should be lenient. Matthew was an avid listener and
had a heart for the poor, as he had also been poor himself.
As a result, Matthew had survived and thrived in a land that
was not always kind to the young, especially one who chose
a profession considered traitorous to his own people. Perhaps
Jehovah, above, would guide him and prevent him from totally
going to the side of the Romans and forgetting who he was and
who his people were—the people of God.

He looked around at the walls of the inn. This was his life,
these walls of stone and mortar. He had started out with a
small house and over the years had expanded his little home
to include four separate rooms, each opening into a central
courtyard, each large enough for several people. A large cooking area in the center of the courtyard was for all to share. The
roof had also been reinforced in order to allow for sleeping up
there in the cool night air.

Tonight the inn was the fullest it had ever been, and far
beyond capacity. The roof was also full and sagging from the
weight. He had forgotten how many were there. The courtyard
was covered with sleeping mats, even into the cooking area,
where there were people against people, some even leaning
against the walls. The building was totally surrounded by tents
and other forms of shelters. There was only one place left in a
corner of the main room, and that he had reserved for himself where the early morning light would reach him from the

window first and awaken him early to start another busy day.

He wondered how the couple was doing in the stable. They had arrived very late in the day and had absolutely nowhere else to go. If that merchant hadn't had to go out and help calm his unruly animals, there would not have been a place for them, even in the stable.

Actually, he had never had a woman stay in the stable. That just wasn't normal practice, and the stable, such as it was, was crowded like everywhere else. In fact, there were several trade caravan drivers already in the stable. But there was no place inside for them, especially with the baby that close to coming. The woman looked like she might already be in labor.

Then there was the other thing about this. All the midwives had also been drawn out of town due to the census. This census had thrown the whole world out of order. This young mother would have to birth the baby by herself with her husband, another thank you to the Romans and their census.

What a stir this census has caused. The Romans had people shifting from here to there instead of counting them where they were living. All this to make sure the Romans were getting their share of the taxes, as if they needed more. But whatever the case, it was good for business. He was getting wealthy; but then, of course, more taxes for the Romans.

His mind returned to the couple in the stable. The carpenter, as he had decided on the trade of the man, looked as if he were competent. Perhaps he could make some repairs at the inn while he was here. After all, the census could take five years or more to finish, and just maybe the price would be less from someone not from this town. It was worth finding out.

Again the innkeeper looked around at the piled humanity he was attempting to host and wondered how anyone could sleep with that much snoring. The whole building shook and rattled at times. What a din! And the odors! He had never smelled that many bodies at one time in one place. It was more than a respectable innkeeper should have to bear. He had heard that this would go on until the Romans had the count they wanted. Oh, well! He was getting wealthy this way, even if the Romans did get more taxes.

The innkeeper settled himself in the little corner he had reserved for himself and tried to go to sleep. But just as he was about to drift into an uncomfortable slumber, he heard a faint sound that startled him into wakefulness again. He strained to locate what he had heard. Then he heard it again, the unmistakable cry of a newborn infant. With a gentle smile of a man full of memories of his own children, the old innkeeper drifted off into an exhausted slumber.

The Old Trader

The old trader had come to this same inn here in this little town of Bethlehem for many years, stopping each time he made a trip to this country. Never in his life had he had a night quite like this. He and his helpers had driven his animals long and hard to reach his destination, and every person and animal was extremely tired from the day's trek.

Knowing the inn would be full, especially with the decree of the Romans to take a census, he had trusted the innkeeper to have a space for him as a regular visitor over many years. Even then he had been relegated to a space in the stable area, with many apologies from the innkeeper.

Many nights of his travels over the years he had slept close to animals and this was not uncomfortable nor an inconvenience to him. The other drivers of his team were camped just outside of town with the many animals used to carry the goods for the market and trading he hoped to accomplish.

He always liked coming to Israel. The land along the routes

he chose to travel was fertile and beautiful, and he almost always received a healthy profit from this market.

He thought, *It would have to happen while he was on the biggest trip of the year. At least the innkeeper was expecting him and had saved room for several of his smaller animals and himself here in the stable.*

If only the Jews wouldn't keep going on about their Messiah! Every year, every trip, he had to listen to the stories they told over and over again. "He will come," they would say, "drive the Romans out of their land, and re-establish the Jewish kingdom over the land Jehovah, God, had given them so long ago.

He would have to be some great Messiah to move these Romans. They were powerful. No one seemed to be able to do anything about them. Oh well. They had given him the freedom to travel and sell his goods. Besides, the Jews were always trying to start some kind of revolt. They were a strange people, these Jews, still believing in a God who they claimed had spoken to them many years before through their fathers, but hadn't spoken to them for over four hundred years. Actually, there are plenty of gods around. Just pick one and you are set, or go without any and you still can get along nicely. But then, tonight...

He had just gotten his animals settled and lain down on his sleeping mat for the night when the innkeeper came into the stable area, disturbing the animals and leading a young man and his very pregnant wife.

In a stable? Normal travelers didn't sleep in stables, especially the women. They slept in the inn or in tents, not here with the animals.

The woman looked extremely tired from traveling, and what's more, she looked like she was about to have the baby any minute. *Here? In a stable? This is not what I need!*

Then just to confirm he was right, the young man approached and asked if it were possible to borrow a blanket to hang over the hollow in the wall of the stable where they had found a space. I wanted no part of this. I gave him two!

He thought, *I know that it was not unusual to have a baby right out in the field, but not here! Not in this stable! Please! Not where I'm trying to sleep!*

The young man thanked the old camel driver profusely and went back to his wife.

What a place for a baby to be born. The stable was alive with the breathing of sweaty animals and the pungent smell of fresh manure. There was little bedding, very little, and of course you had to pay extra for it.

The niches where a person could sleep were nothing more than hollowed out places in the wall, about two hand's-breadth above the floor in order to keep the urine run-off out of the places for the sleeping mats. Of course, there was always one of the animals who would manage to get a bite of a blanket and pull. That always brought cursing from the victim, and laughter from everyone else who was more than happy it was not their turn.

I was right! She is having the baby! I wasn't even there when my own children were born. Why should I be? That was for women. Oh, well. Maybe now I can get some sleep.

Things had just finally gotten quiet in the stable when once again the animals were stirred and awakened. This time by a group of grungy shepherds. They came running into the stable like there was a fire and asking where the baby was. Now the whole stable was awake. Some of those who had been sleeping began cursing. Others began shaking their fists and throwing pieces of manure or chunks of dirt at the shepherds.

Then the baby's father stepped out from behind the blanket and quietly led the shepherds to his wife sitting next to the manger, where he could see the baby lying.

As he watched from his sleeping place he thought, *Those crazy shepherds! They got down on their knees right in the manure! I guess that goes to show that shepherds really are a low class, especially if they are from this country. And are they praising their god?*

Finally the shepherds left and it again became quiet, as quiet as a stable could be.

The camel driver lay on his mat wide awake thinking about all he had seen and heard.

The thing that really bothered me was what they were saying as they left. They thought this baby was their long-awaited Messiah. Now I know these Jews are crazy. What Messiah would be born in a stable? Wait...

How did they know there was a baby born here?

Tonight?

In this particular stable?

And why did they call him the Messiah?

As the old camel driver lay there wondering and questioning the things that had happened, peace settled over the little stable in Bethlehem. Sleep slowly came to the animals, then to the drivers, and even to the new mother, worn by the travail of childbirth. And at last, sleep came even to the old camel driver.

Only the baby's father, standing quietly, could not sleep as he looked at the new infant in awe and wonder, remembering all the things he had been told and all that had happened leading to this night. As he stood there in the quiet darkness of the stable, he pondered what the future would hold for this special child.

FROM THE BIBLE IN THE BOOK OF LUKE
LUKE CHAPTER 2, VERSES 1 THROUGH 7 (ESV)

In those days a decree went out from Caeser Agustus that all the world should be registered.

This was the first registration when Quirinius was governor of Syria. And all went to be registered, each to his own town. And Joseph also went up from Galilee, from the town of Nazareth, to Judea, to the city of David, which is called Bethlehem, because he was of the house and lineage of David, to be registered with Mary, his betrothed, who was with child. And while they were there, the time came for her to give birth. And she gave birth to her firstborn son and wrapped him in swaddling clothes and laid him in a manger, because there was no place for them in the inn.

The First Sighting

The moon was half past its evening visit when the king rose from his sleeping place and left his chamber to walk on the balcony and gaze at the night sky. It had been a particularly grueling day, and he had ridden long and hard just to be in his own rooms when evening fell.

The campaign to restore peace to a rebellious region had taken its toll on his energy and the energy of his soldiers, and the desire to be home had pushed him and his men to the maximum limits of their endurance.

Then, when everything had been put in its place and his servants were at peace in their quarters or homes, he had finally laid down to rest, but sleep just would not come. No matter how he tried or even how long he laid there, his eyes were still wide open looking for something he could not describe.

His reign as high king had been a successful one, but as with all kingdoms, there had been the never-ending uprisings of first one tribe and then another. As soon as one quieted down, another would start somewhere else. Even though his reign had been a relatively quiet one, it had never been entirely at rest. He had tried. Someday perhaps there would be a king that would be able to rule in perfect peace. He certainly had not been able to do it.

As the king walked, he glanced around behind him. *Yes, Agbar was there. Agbar was always there, just waiting to be asked to do something. Even rising in the middle of the night could not escape the attention of this faithful one.*

The king had never had a servant that he trusted so much, especially one who was a captured slave. In fact, it was often said that Agbar knew more about the king than the king knew about himself. But, he was always there when the king needed him and the king trusted him completely, even with his life.

Agbar was not his original name. The king did not even know what it had been. Agbar was just the name the king used and it had stuck to the slave, from the day he had been purchased at the market. He was now known as Agbar to all.

Agbar was from the land of the Hebrews, a Jew, and a former priest in his nation's religion, a belief that the king knew nothing about. He did know that Agbar practiced his beliefs in the privacy of his own quarters, but the king never questioned him about them. What he believed was his own business and as long as his duties were carried out, the king didn't care what god he worshipped.

The king turned back to his walking and then suddenly stopped. There in the dark sky right before him was a star.

It wasn't there a few moments ago, or was it?

It was very large and bright, and stood out from all the other stars. In fact, it almost dominated the entire sky with its presence. He was unable to take his eyes off of it.

The king called to his servant. "Agbar. Do you see that star?" the king asked. "I have never seen it before."

The servant came obediently to the king's side and looked to where the king was pointing.

There in the sky before them was a star of incredible brightness and beauty. It seemed to stand out from the other stars and appeared to be close enough that he could reach out and touch it with his hand. There was also a feeling that came when he looked at it that made him want to go to it somehow. It actually felt like it was pulling him towards it.

"That star must be for a new king; perhaps the king of the world," said the king to Agbar. "Only the greatest king to ever live could own a star like that. Perhaps it is time for the true "King of Peace" of the old prophecies."

He turned to Agbar who was staring at the star, speechless, with his mouth open. "Go at once and call the wise men from all the provinces!" the king commanded. "I must learn what this star is about and who it honors. We must also prepare gifts to bring me into his favor."

The servant did not move but stood, still as a stone, and continued to stare at the star.

"Go!" the king commanded a second time.

This time, Agbar turned and ran from the room, stopping only for the customary three bows, then running out the door with his robe flying. He left the door wide open, something that was not customarily done, and never by a servant, especially by the king's personal servant; nor did the king's personal servant ever run.

The king looked at the open door for a moment, wondering what had gotten into his servant who had never reacted in that way before, and then turned back to the beautiful star.

What kind of gift could he send to this new king? What gift could be worthy of his highest majesty? What gift could bestow enough honor on a king so high and mighty?

Deep in thought, the king turned from the star and slowly went back to his bedchamber.

It was long before he fell into sleep.

The Youngest Shepherd

The stars seemed unusually bright in the dark quiet sky as the shepherds began settling down for the night. The sheep had calmed down quickly and were lying here and there, all within the sight of the group of shepherds who were in charge of their care. It had been a peaceful day and the shepherds were in a jovial mood, laughing and joking with one another as men do when their work had gone well. They were also training a new young boy by the name of Nathan, who actually was the grandson of the oldest shepherd in the group. Just nine years old, this was Nathan's first week with the flock. He was a quick learner and liked by all the other shepherds.

Grandfather, as he was addressed by all, had been a shepherd all his life from the time he was a boy and had gone through the new shepherd training just as Nathan was doing now.

Grandfather had taken his profession seriously and from the beginning had the reputation of never losing a member of the flock to a wild animal while under his care. It was for this reason he had been chosen to oversee the flock that was being held for the temple sacrifices in Jerusalem.

The training time for a young boy who would become a shepherd was also a time for the older men to share memories, especially the history of their families and the history of the nation of Israel. This was also the time that the laws given by "Jehovah", their God, were passed on and memorized.

Since there were no books and scrolls available for the common people, the nation's learning—both of the past and the promise of the future—came entirely from the passing of information from person to person. This was one of the primary duties of fathers and grandfathers to share with their sons and grandsons. The time around the evening campfire was a perfect time for this to take place.

Tonight was no exception, as Grandfather had agreed to tell again the story of the promised Messiah. Nathan never tired of hearing it the way Grandfather told it. "It was the promise of Jehovah," Grandfather would say, "And when Jehovah promises, it is only a matter of time, Jehovah's time, before the promise will be fulfilled."

The sheep were calm, the other shepherds were laying out their mats, and Nathan was waiting impatiently for Grandfather to take his place at the fire. "You are the last shepherd of your family line," Grandfather had told him over and over, "and it will be your responsibility to carry on this story to your grandchildren."

Nathan was the youngest of his family and the only boy of seven children. He was now being trained to watch and care for sheep, just as had many boys through previous generations.

Even father Abraham had been a shepherd, and Nathan was proud to be a shepherd like the famous father of the nation of Israel.

He looked up the gentle slopes toward the small city of Bethlehem, but all he could see was the outline of the town against the night sky, the town that was called the "City of David".

"Yes," said Grandfather, joining Nathan at the fire and looking also with Nathan at Bethlehem, not too far away, its dark shadow standing out against the night sky. "You know the Messiah will come from the House of David as I have often told you."

It was just at that moment that the night world exploded into light. The darkness of the sky was suddenly replaced by a creature unlike anything Nathan had ever seen. The creature glowed so brightly that Nathan had to squint his eyes almost closed in order to see. He looked through his almost closed eyelids at the other shepherds to confirm what he was seeing. The others could see only what was visible from under their blankets and mats where they were hiding and carefully peeking out. They were terrified and tried to lie as still as stones.

Then the creature spoke and the sound shook the skies like thunder. Still Nathan could make out clearly the words the creature was saying to them and seemingly to the whole world.

"Fear not! For behold, I bring you good news of great joy that will be for all the people. For unto you is born this day in the city of David a Savior who is Christ the Lord."

Nathan stood and stared while the creature, who had to be an angel, delivered the rest of the message.

"And this will be a sign for you: you will find a baby wrapped in swaddling cloths and lying in a manger."

And suddenly there was with the angel a multitude of heavenly host praising God and saying, "Glory to God in the highest, and on earth peace among those with whom he is pleased!"

All of them were singing, making the skies and the whole world ring with their song.

There must have been millions of them. The sight was so incredibly beautiful, but also totally overwhelming and terrifying. Nathan had never seen or heard anything like it. He could do nothing but just stand there and stare and listen.

But then, just as suddenly as they had appeared, the creatures were gone. The skies were silent again.

Slowly the shepherds crawled out from under their blankets and looked at each other to see if they were alone in what they had seen and heard, or perhaps were they all as a group dreaming. It was totally quiet for a few minutes as the shepherds gathered their wits about them and tried to understand what had just happened. They looked at each other and then turned to look around at the night sky and the dark fields and hills.

"It must be!" Grandfather said, finally breaking the silence. "This must be the one we have been waiting for."

"But in a stable?" asked one shepherd.

"Wrapped as a common baby?" asked another.

"I don't know about that, but I do think we need to go and see this child," said Grandfather.

"All I know is that if this is the Messiah, I don't want to miss Him."

"But we dare not leave the sheep!" said another almost as old as Grandfather.

"That is true," Grandfather agreed. "The youngest will have to stay." He turned to look at Nathan as he spoke. "You will stay with the sheep while we go to see this child. In the morning perhaps you can go."

Nathan watched as the others started up the long hill toward the city, and then as they began to run, robes flying as if they could not get there fast enough. Soon they were lost to sight in the darkness.

Nathan gave up looking after the others and turned again to the night sky. It was just as it had been earlier when Grandfather was getting ready to tell the story of the Messiah. It was as if nothing had happened, except...

Nathan looked again. He did not remember the one bright star he now saw. He didn't think it was there before. He was sure he would remember one so bright.

Nathan looked around at the flocks he was now watching by himself. The sheep were absolutely still and sleeping as if nothing had happened. They had not even moved at the appearance of the creatures and their singing.

Why? That was not the normal way of sheep. It took very little to alarm a flock of this size, but not a single sound or movement had they made.

Why?

Nathan sat and pondered the events that had just taken place. What he had just seen and heard would never be erased from his mind. The events that had just happened were forever burned into his memory. He could only just sit and listen in his mind, over and over, to the message that had been spoken to the shepherds.

Nathan was still sitting that way when the others came back from the city of Bethlehem, singing and praising God in a way that would wake bodies in their tombs if that were possible.

They told Nathan what they had seen in the town that night. The baby in the manger, the baby's mother, her husband, just as the angel had told them. Nathan listened to every word, storing it in his memory. He would never forget this night. It was locked in his mind forever.

It seemed like a very long time before they began to quiet down and even longer before the last of them had gone to sleep. Nathan was already fast asleep on his mat, totally exhausted from the excitement he had experienced.

All too shortly morning came, and Nathan seemed to be the last one up as Grandfather shook him awake, saying it was time to move the sheep. Nathan got up quickly, thinking about the baby in Bethlehem, when Grandfather said it was time to go find another pasture.

The herd began to move away from the city. Nathan looked at Grandfather expectantly, but Grandfather just shook his head and said, "I'm sorry, but you know these sheep are for the sin sacrifice at the temple in Jerusalem They must be kept well fed and cared for so they may be offered in a manner according to the law. This field has been grazed as long as we can."

Disappointed, Nathan turned to follow the sheep that in turn followed the singing of Grandfather as he led them to new pasture. As Nathan started over the crest of the hill, he turned once more to look back at the city of Bethlehem. All he could see against the morning sunrise was the outline of the city of David where the Messiah was to be born.

With a quiet sigh, Nathan turned and walked down the hill after the sheep.

FROM THE BIBLE IN THE BOOK OF LUKE
LUKE CHAPTER 2, VERSES 8 THROUGH 20 (ESV)

And in the same region there were shepherds out in the field, keeping watch over their flock by night. And an angel of the Lord appeared to them, and the glory of the Lord shone around them and they were filled with great fear. And the angel said to them, "Fear not, for behold, I bring you good news of great joy that will be for all the people. For unto you is born this day in the city of David a Savior, who is Christ the Lord. And this will be a sign for you; you will find a baby wrapped in swaddling cloths and lying in a manger." And suddenly, there was with the angel a multitude of the heavenly host praising God and saying,

> *Glory to God in the highest,*
> *and on earth, peace among those*
> *with whom He is pleased!"*

When the angels went away from them into heaven, the shepherds said to one another, "Let us go over to Bethlehem and see this thing that has happened, which the Lord has made known to us. And they went with haste and found Mary and Joseph, and the baby lying in a manger. And when they saw it, they made known the saying that had been told them concerning this child. And all who heard it wondered at what the shepherds told them. But Mary treasured up all these things, pondering them in her heart. And the shepherds returned, glorifying and praising God, for all they had heard and seen, as it had been told them.

Caleb

My name is Caleb. I am eight years old and the youngest of seven. My father died of a sickness two years ago and my mother is still trying to find ways to feed all of us. Some of my siblings are able to help. My older brother died with the sickness that took my father. Three sisters are married. Two sisters and I are left at home. We live in this small town of Bethlehem, a town named in the prophets for something very important to happen in the future, but I don't know of anything that has come of those promises yet. Whatever it is that is supposed to happen is still in the future and I don't even know for sure what it is.

My parents named me after a man of old, Caleb, said to be a hero of our tribe. "It is an honor to carry this name," my father had said to me, "so carry it well."

My father would then remind me of the man, Caleb, who went after the giants in the land when he was eighty years old and conquered them in order to claim his tribe's inheritance. I would listen to what he was telling me but I could never quite see any giants for me to conquer except in my dreams.

Since I am the youngest, sometimes I am almost forgotten when we gather around the evening meal, especially with sisters wanting to talk and share. A side benefit of this is that I can disappear to find things to do that I want to do but shouldn't, and skip out on an occasional chore when I think I can get away with it.

This was what happened one of the nights during the time of the "Census" when our little town was overflowing with travelers from all over the nation. I didn't even know for sure what a census was, but it made everyone go somewhere and a lot of them came here to Bethlehem, the "City of David."(David was another of our country's great heroes, the greatest king ever).

My mother and sisters were asleep on their mats while I was wide awake, moving about the quiet town, thinking about the many people who were here, crowding every nook and corner. The innkeeper had so many people that he had them lying all over the floor, wall to wall. This had never happened before like this or for so long. There were so many animals gathered in temporary pens I was not able to count them. There were people sleeping on the rooftops, in tents, and even on mats out in the open or under a tree.

I was surprised when one couple who came in close to the going down of the sun found a place in the stable of the inn. The stable for this inn was just a large inset, or cave, in the side of the hill. There was room in this natural cave for a small number of people and just a few larger insets in the walls where a person or persons could sleep above the ground level. The animals would lie outside on the ground. Outside the front of the cave were several large circles made of posts and limbs which made up the rest of the stable and the extra area needed while the census was being done. These were connected to the rock walls on either side of the opening of the cave. I had watched with fascination as all of this was being built and made ready for the overload of people coming to the "City of David".

When you are eight years old and no one is really watching you, there is much to see and learn and store up in your mind for future reference.

I had made friends with the innkeeper, who always had a snack for an ever hungry boy. I saw soldiers coming and going at strange times. I also made friends with the tax collector who was just a few years older than I and spent his time at the gate collecting money. My mother had told me not to talk to him, but you know how I treated that order; I talked with him every chance I got. He was not much older than me and had lost both his parents to the same sickness that had taken my father and brother, so we had something in common. We also had a mutual friend in the innkeeper, and the three of us shared a special bond and all the news we could gather from our very different lives.

But back to that night. I was curious about the man and his wife and why they would even consider sleeping in the stable; the man would, perhaps, but not the woman. The part of the stable that was the cave area at least had some cover so maybe they wanted to be under some protection as the woman was very large with a baby.

I went first to the inn to see what I could learn. I found the innkeeper concentrating on putting things back in order after a very busy evening and getting ready for the next day. It was plain he had far too much to do and absolutely no time for an idle news chat. Judging from the mats covering the floor of the main room, there was also no room for me to even help.

Next I went by to see if the tax collector was still up, but there was no sign of activity at his house. I decided to go on back to my own mat and get some sleep. The way to my home led past the stable of the inn. As I began to pass by some of the rock wall pens added to the fences, I stopped to look at the mass of animals lying close to the opening of the cave, and as I stood there I heard soft voices. They sounded like a man's low soft pitches and a woman's higher voice, but very soft so that others would not be disturbed. With my curiosity aroused, I quietly stepped closer to see who was speaking.

I was just about to peek around the back of a group of sheep when the woman gave a soft cry. I stopped and remained motionless, trying to decide about what I should do—go or stay—when I heard the cry of a newborn baby.

Realizing I had been an uninvited hearing witness to a birth, I crept back to the entrance of the stable, and as silently as possible walked away. I had been around birth before, but only with my own relatives. I suddenly felt like an intruder.

I moved away from the stable and wandered down the center way of the town. As I slowly went along, I looked up at the night sky, full of joy inside at what I had just heard. There was something about a new baby that was exciting to me. I couldn't put it into words, but now I was again too awake to think about sleep.

Then, from the edge of town, I heard the sound of running feet. Suddenly, around the corner of the last house, the shepherds who had been watching the flocks of sheep on the hillside outside of town appeared. They had their robes tucked up in their arms and were running as fast as they could run. They flew by me and did not even notice me in their haste. I turned as they sped by and I was surprised to see that they went right to the stable I had just left, the stable where the baby had been born.

Of course this was too much for me to leave alone. I turned and followed the shepherds back to the stable, and this time I did not hide carefully but joined the shepherds as if I were one of them, but staying at the back of the group. They looked in every circle and corner of the makeshift stable and stopped when they looked behind the hanging blanket. Here they found the mother, father, and a baby in the manger.

The young mother, embarrassed at the attention she and the baby were suddenly receiving, lifted the baby from the manger and held the tiny bundle high so all could see. The shepherds, every one of them, suddenly went to their knees right there in the middle of the stable. For a long while the shepherds stayed on their knees, alternating between staring at the baby and then bowing their heads to the ground murmuring. I could barely hear their words. They were all speaking and singing psalms and words of praise to Jehovah God on High for His promises.

My mind was trying to take it all in. Why would they act this way around a baby?

I looked around for Nathan, a boy about my age who I knew

was with the shepherds and was being trained by his grandfather and the other shepherds to care for a flock of sheep, but I saw no sign of him. I had hoped he could tell me what this was all about. I wondered why he was not here; he would surely know something! I looked for Nathan's grandfather, who was the one in charge of the flock. I finally saw him right up front as close to the baby as he could get. He also was just as the others, kneeling and bowing and murmuring quiet words I could barely make out.

Finally, the shepherd band slowly began rising to their feet and moving toward the outer edge of the stable enclosure. They remained quiet and pensive as they left the stable and turned in the direction from where they had appeared so suddenly. They started slowly down the town's central street almost without a sound and with heads bowed.

But, then, as they reached the edge of town, the shepherds lost their sense of quietness and began singing and shouting at the top of their voices. And now they were saying something else. They were shouting, "THE MESSIAH HAS COME! THE MESSIAH HAS COME!" It was like they were trying to tell the whole world.

They kept that up all the way out of town as they headed back to their fields and their flocks. I watched until they were out of sight around the end of the line of houses and the tents on the edge of town. People were awakened by the din and were at their windows and doorways yelling back at the group. Some of the shepherds had stopped to tell those who would listen about the angel's visit. It was a while before all quieted down and Bethlehem returned to the normal stillness of the night.

My mind was in a state of wonderment as I walked home, storing another strange happening in my young memory. I lay on my mat trying to organize everything into something in a way that would make sense, but I could only see a huge jumble of confusing parts I was unable to put together. Lying there, I planned who I would ask about these things in the morning. I finally fell asleep, my mind spinning like a desert whirlwind.

I woke very early and dressed quickly. It was my daily job to run errands for the innkeeper in exchange for my morning food. This I did gladly as I always seemed to be hungry. I made my way hurriedly to the inn where the innkeeper was busy and as was his habit, awake long before me. He welcomed me with a smile and gave me a loaf of bread and drink.

"Take these to the couple in the stable," he said. "They will be tired and hungry; and tell them there will be no cost for this."

He looked at me and told me he had a very soft place in his heart for a new family just starting out with their first child.

I went out to the stable and worked my way between the animals to where the couple with the new baby was up and starting to prepare for wherever they were bound for that day. I went up to the father and handed him the parcel of food the innkeeper had sent. When I told him the innkeeper's message of no cost he looked surprised, then smiled and said, "The Lord has supplied our need."

I walked away back to start my next errand and planning who I would begin asking about all these things I had experienced. I think the Rabbi will be the first person I will ask.

The Centurion's Story

The centurion was trying to make sense of the night guard's report. What would make a group of shepherds leave their flocks in the middle of the night and come running to a stable here in town, only to leave shortly afterward singing and dancing as if they were trying to wake the dead, if that were possible? Sometimes he just did not understand these people. He had established this house in Bethlehem for a place to take a break from the constant noise of Jerusalem. Even here he had soldiers stopping by for orders.

A quiet knock sounded at the door and the Centurion leaned back in his chair as his aide showed a messenger into the area he was using as an office. The messenger approached the desk, saluted smartly, and held out a roll of papyrus, tied and sealed.

"I was told by my commander to make very few stops on the way and to give this to you personally," the soldier said.

The Centurion looked at the messenger and noticed the travel stains on his uniform.

"Where are you stationed?" he asked.

The messenger replied, "At the garrison close to Nazareth. I was instructed to reach you as soon as possible."

"That's a long ride," the centurion said. The centurion signaled to his aide. "See to this man's needs; food, and a place to sleep. See also to the care of the horse."

The Centurion waved for the messenger to be dismissed.

The aide saluted and turned to go. The messenger followed suit and they left, closing the door behind them.

The Centurion looked at the message in his hand and then looked again. Beside the seal was a signature he had not seen for over two years, the mark of his own son, Marcus.

With hurried shaking hands he untied the ribbon, broke the seal, and unrolled the letter.

Dearest father,

I have waited to write to you until I knew for sure where I would be assigned. Three months ago I was promoted to Centurion. I asked to be stationed in Israel, hoping I would be close enough to at least visit you on occasion. I am assigned over the unit near a small town called Nazareth, two days' strong ride from your garrison. I have been here only 30 days and was able to move into the last commander's lodging.

I did need to have some furniture built and was able to find a carpenter who had enough time to complete the things I needed before he, too, was leaving to go to the city of his ancestors to be counted for the census. The carpenter, Joseph by name, completed the

pieces in a short time and the work was quite satis-
factory. The Jews were not using him very much as
these people seem to draw away from someone who
stumbles about their "righteous living". It seems that
his wife was found to be pregnant before they were
married. I am happy he got my work finished before
they left.

Mother sends her love as do my sisters and younger
brother. All are well and look forward to your return
next year for a visit. They miss you, as do I.

I hope to be able to come to you as soon as my
affairs are in order. Apparently Nazareth seems not
to be the home of any notable ancestor, so this town
at least just goes on as usual. It seems quite peaceful
here. A few of the people, like Joseph and his wife,
have left to be counted for the census.

I hope this writing finds you in good health and
well-being.

Your son, Marcus

The centurion read the letter again and then leaned back
in his chair as memories of the past floated through his mind.
For a time he just sat that way remembering his son as a small
child.

He had visited Nazareth a few months ago to correct a
military problem with the nearby garrison and had not in
the furthest stretch of his imagination dreamed that his
eldest son, Marcus, would be taking over the work he had
accomplished there. He understood the challenge of finding

a quality carpenter, as it seemed this census was turning the whole world upside down. Actually, he needed one to do some work for his rooms here but had not found one since he had purchased this house here in Bethlehem; that is until today. His aide had mentioned that he had just this evening seen a man with carpentry tools arrive in the town, and with a very pregnant wife. This man would need work. He would have his aide search out this carpenter.

In fact, he thought with growing excitement, the work could be done next week while he delivered the answer to his son's letter in person. He rose to his feet and began pacing the room while making plans for the two-day trip to Nazareth.

Morning Water

It was the way of life that the women of the town would daily take time to gather at the well to draw water for the house, and of course, they made it a time when all the other women could take a break from their duties of the home and the tasks required there.

Because the only well in the town was deep, there was plenty of time between taking turns working the crank to lift the buckets of water for the stories that were part of everyday living. It was also the way of the women to share things their husbands had shared with them, or things they had heard from a merchant or traveler as they passed through the town. It was always enjoyable to hear and share tidings from distant relatives who might be staying for a few days with them.

With the census, these times of hosting were much extended, but the customs of this land and people were still practiced; a home must always be open to host traveling family members and distant relatives. Because of this, many times the women of the town were better versed in the happenings of other parts of the country and extended family members than their husbands, because they heard more and seemed more comfortable with sharing the details of all they knew and learning the details of all they did not know. The men's work, especially those who cared for the flocks of sheep, would keep the man of the house away for long periods of time, as they had to continually move to areas of good grazing. These times could even turn into weeks, so there was always time spent sharing news and information among the family members gathered around meals when the men were home.

But, at the well in the water-drawing time of the day, the men were not present and the women were free and even eager to share with other women. It was time for news they had gathered, and their personal opinions, some of which were those they had not been able to express openly at home because of listening children. There were also those opinions that the men didn't need to hear, or want to hear.

This day the statements, questions, and answers flew fast and furiously.

"Did you hear the shepherds yelling in the street last night?"

"Yes, but I didn't see where they were going, they passed by so fast."

"I heard them. They went to the stable at the inn."

"What's there to see in a stable?"

"A baby was born there."

"Last night?"

"Yes. I heard its cry."

"Why? In that stinky place? Ugghh"

"I would have found a better place."

"Me too."

"What were the parents thinking?"

"But why were the shepherds there?"

"Who knows?"

"Who were the parents?"

"Nobody knows. They're not from here."

"Where then?"

"Don't know. Just here for the census like everyone else."

"Well! That will go on forever."

"As long as it takes the Romans to get their count for taxes."

"Did you hear what the shepherds were yelling and shouting?"

"Yes, I heard them twice. Once going this way quietly and then the second time when they came back the other way when they started yelling."

"Did they leave their sheep?"

"I couldn't quite make out what they were yelling, but I did hear part of a Psalm."

"A Psalm? Is that all they were saying?"

"No. There was another thing they were yelling. To me it sounded like someone had come."

"Who was coming?"

"I heard the words but they made no sense."

"What did it sound like?"

"It sounded like, 'The Messiah has come'."

"What? Messiah? Are you sure? Here?"

"In a stable?"

"A stinky stable."

"That's what they said."

"Those shepherds have lost their senses!"

"Careful; remember, some of those shepherds are our husbands."

"There is an old prophesy about a Messiah, but I don't remember all of it."

"Well, they were to move to a new pasture today so it will be a few days before we can get the truth of it."

"Well, sitting out there in the fields for days, they can come up with some pretty good tales. It will be interesting to hear this one."

"It will have to be good. Shepherds walking away from their sheep in the middle of the night could be trouble for them."

"And that means trouble for us."

"What is the old story about the Messiah anyway?"

"Something about a new king; one that will last forever, from the line of David."

"Forever? How is that going to happen?"

"I don't know. My husband tried to tell me one day. It is somewhere in the old prophesies. I'll ask him when he gets home this next time."

"I'll ask mine also. He has also talked about it."

"Mine too."

"Me too."

"I'd better check on my bread."

"Me too."

The well again became quiet, waiting for the next day's gathering.

The Rabbi of Bethlehem

The Rabbi leaned back on his stool, looking at the stacks and bundles of scrolls piled on the table before him, considering each one and trying to decide which writing to examine next.

Where would he find the answer to the questions that had plagued his mind since the night when a baby was born in the innkeeper's stable and the shepherds had left their flocks to come running into town to see? Then they had left the town singing and shouting about the Messiah. Could this baby be connected to the old stories and prophesies? There were so many words of promise that had been kept through the years of history, and about the history of this people. There were also the prophets and their promises of a Messiah given through them by Jehovah for his people.

He sought through his memory to see if he could find a clue as to where he should start next. He so wanted to believe what his mind was starting to tell him but he needed to confirm what his soul, deep inside, had already come to believe.

Was this it! Was this the promise his people and this land had waited for since the founding of the nation? Had he come—the long promised Messiah; Shiloh; the Prince of eternal Peace? Was this the right time? The right place?

He thought of the constant presence of regular patrols of Roman soldiers passing by on the roads exhibiting their power and authority over the land. Was it possible? Why now? When the Romans ruled the known world; when so many of his nation's people were scattered all over the many countries; when so many had given up on God and no longer believed that He cared or even existed. Hundreds of years, so many different kingdoms, so many wars, so many dead, all fighting to rule this land; but only one long ago promise from that great, one and only eternal God.

Deep in his soul he wanted to believe. He wanted to accept all he had heard. But he also felt the need to confirm these things with the ancient writings and prophesies of the past.

He must gather all the facts together before he took this to the Sanhedrin. They would not listen if he did not have the evidence of what he was saying. Long ago he had been part of the Sanhedrin in Jerusalem and they knew him as a man of wisdom and careful study. But this—this was above anything outside of the current and common thoughts and beliefs and far beyond anything they would easily accept. They would be skeptical, even with the scripture in front of them. He had to be absolutely sure before daring to share the joyful news of the fulfillment of the most important and long-awaited prophecy of history, that of the Messiah.

The old Rabbi was part of a long lineage of priests spanning many generations of the tribe of Levi. He had served Jehovah faithfully in several synagogues and had at last served in the High Counsel in the city of Jerusalem. He decided to come to this small town and synagogue several years ago when his years of age were great and when he felt that he was beginning to slow down and believed himself unable to handle the demands of the large city synagogue and the great number of people under his charge.

Once here, he soon saw the choice was a good one. He had always been a good listener and with his gentle spirit and loving heart, the old man had quickly become an integral part of the community, trusted and loved by all. Even the young boys he taught at the synagogue school each morning had grown close to him and studied together as a tightly woven robe. They would run to greet him as he walked down the street each morning and would share their discoveries and opinions with him and each other as they grew in their studies.

The street had actually become another classroom while walking each morning to the synagogue. This relationship was very important as the boys were expected to enter the world of manhood at the age of 13. His time with them was limited, and he strove to share with them everything he could while they were his to teach. The parents of his students were grateful to have a teacher of his quality in front of the boys of this small town.

He would also go out among the people wherever they were working and visit with them, listening and quietly receiving many pieces of input which helped him understand and guide these people for whom God had chosen him to be a help and comfort in their daily lives.

He picked up another scroll and began reading again, but even as he read, his mind could not move very far from his memories of the shouts of the shepherds the night before. "The Messiah has come! The Messiah has come!" they had shouted to the sky above. "The angels told us and we believe because now we also have seen him."

That was the same story the young boy, Caleb, had brought to him that next morning about that which he had seen and heard in the stable.

Caleb was a fountain of information. He freely ran the streets at night, having lost his father to a sickness. The Rabbi had gone to the innkeeper when Caleb's father had died and convinced the innkeeper to give Caleb's mother work and food to help. The old Rabbi also contributed to their stores, but through the innkeeper so as to stay neutral to the others in the town and away from any gossip.

The stories Caleb had brought to the old Rabbi that morning had astounded the Rabbi to the point that he himself went to find out what had started the young boy's tale. He had begun with the innkeeper, then gone to find the shepherds, which turned into a long walk as they had changed fields for better feeding, then to the young tax collector, who the Rabbi had also befriended.

Nathan, the young tax collector, worked for the hated Romans but had also earned the respect of his townspeople by being fair and gentle with his dealings. He also went out to the camping place of the camel caravan of traders just outside of the town but they had left early in the morning, continuing their travel, so he was not able to confirm Caleb's mention of a camel driver in the stable. But as Caleb was not in the habit of telling untruths, he decided he would accept what he had been told as fact.

Finally, coming back to his room, he sat for hours just trying to put everything together and praying for an answer. He then again started looking through the scrolls in the small library this synagogue had. As each of his thoughts became real and more confirmed one by one, the rabbi would stop and meditate on each new fact and place it in order where he felt it belonged. The total picture was starting to take shape and his amazement and excitement continued to grow as he kept on working. Was this the time Jehovah had chosen to fulfill His promise?

He also began wondering how he would present this to the chief priests and Rabbis in Jerusalem. They had lost the vision of the promised Messiah. The Romans had total control of the country, but had allowed the priests to continue in their beliefs and practices as long as they did not run contrary to Roman law or start some kind of rebellion among the people.

The priests had tried to adjust their beliefs to the Romans' demands in order to keep themselves on the Romans' good side, but by doing so had actually altered the country's traditional beliefs. This also had the effect of watering down the truths that had been given so long ago by God, and had squelched the hope the spiritual leaders were to maintain through every generation. To present this would take some careful planning.

There were two people he had not talked to yet, and that must be his next visit. He was going to visit the parents and see the baby for himself. At this thought his heart began to beat faster. He rose from his bench and began preparing himself for his visit to the newly born Messiah.

His heart was still beating very fast and now his breath was also becoming more difficult.

He suddenly felt fatigue wash over him and decided perhaps it would be best to take a few moments of rest before going to see this child.

He lay back down on his mat for a short nap, asking Jehovah again to confirm the truth he was now accepting.

It was then he heard Jehovah calling for him to come home.

Part 3

Bethlehem

The Seers

There were fourteen dominions, each guided by a sub-monarch, united under the high king. Each sub-monarch had personal advisors, aged and experienced, considered to be the most learned and wisest in the ways of their respective dominions. They were called seers and were held in high esteem by their own people and the other seers in similar positions across the kingdom of the high king.

These seers had been called to a meeting of great importance by the servant of the high king of their land, a slave called Agbar. The reason for the meeting had not been announced.

These seers were known to one another, as they often met in groups of three and four according to need and location of their particular dominions. But to meet together on this scale was a most unusual occasion. This was either a national emergency or a proclamation of major importance.

Each seer wore a head covering indicating their particular culture and location, and also the level of importance of the office they held. These head coverings were of a turban style and were never removed when in public as that was considered a disgrace. They were also an indication to the leaders and all other people of how they should be addressed, and in many cases, how low the bow should be when approached.

Within this group, however, there was also a hierarchy of respect that was observed. This was primarily represented by the presence of the senior seer referred to only as "Old One". No one knew him by name. No one knew how old he was nor addressed him by any other title than "Old One." Even all the other seers bowed low when he approached or when he was approached.

His words, when spoken, were revered and considered absolute. Because Old One was to be at this meeting, the others were much concerned as they tried to come up with a possible reason for their call. His presence suggested something of great importance.

When the seers began arriving at the king's palace, Agbar was in charge of getting them situated in their lodgings and seeing to their needs and wants as much as each required. Old One, of course received the location closest to the great meeting hall in which all was to be brought to light. His room was also the most beautiful of all the guest rooms in the high king's palace. All the rooms prepared for the seers were fabulously furnished and decorated to a level just below that of the high king, of course.

When all were settled in and all preparations in proper readiness, the king himself would present his reason for calling this gathering of the great minds.

The meeting was to be held in the great meeting room which also housed the king's library. In the center of this great room sat a huge table around which were low benches and cushions normal for that time, and mats for reclining. Behind the cushions and mats were other tables covered with every kind of food known. This bounty was for the purpose of satisfying the individual tastes of these special guests.

Behind the benches and tables, waiting, were numerous servants, there to care for their assigned seer, and to see that none of the seers' wishes were unsatisfied. It was custom for the seers to bring their own personal servants, for they alone knew the special needs and wishes of their masters.

Around this seemingly cavernous room were walls of open shelves, ledges and indentations in the walls holding an immense number of stone tablets and papyrus scrolls collected over many years by this kingdom and its kings. It was a formidable library, and meeting here only added to the questions already in the minds of the seers.

The king's arrival was set for the evening shortly after dark, but no one understood why this particular time was chosen. When the time did draw near, everyone, including servants, were in the great hall in their proper place, waiting anxiously in their best dress and head coverings, anticipating the time they would be given the reason they had been summoned.

At last the sound of the king's entourage was heard down the long halls and everyone did a last minute check to make sure all was in proper readiness. The great door swung open and the king appeared, but not in his normal royal dress for visiting dignitaries, but in the clothing he wore for working every day with his staff.

Bewildered, the seers looked at each other but kept their silence as the king made ready to speak. That came only after the king gave a long slow look around the table and took a short moment to search each face. The high king was familiar with every one of these seers, having met them in his travels across his kingdom.

This king had great respect for these men and trusted that they would be able to provide the answers he sought. But instead of sitting in the high king's place, he began, "Friends and honored guides of our kingdom. After a long ride home from the northern area of the kingdom, I stepped out to get some air as I was unable to sleep. When I looked up into the night sky, I saw a sight that was like no other I have ever seen; a star of unusual beauty and brightness as never has been seen before. My servant also witnessed this sight and now I ask you to also step outside with me to the balcony and see this star for yourself."

The king then turned and led the way to the large doors opening to a broad porch which was open to the night sky. The star the king had seen was still in the same location as it was when it had first appeared.

The seers had all left their places and followed the king onto the balcony. As each man came into sight of the star, he stopped, and then moved very slowly farther onto the balcony. The others pushed out the door to join them, and then moved carefully as if they might disturb the vision they were seeing before them. Soon they were all staring at the star.

No words were spoken; the sight of the star needed no words.

The servants, who also had listened to the king's presentation to the seers, were crowded together in a tightly huddled group around the inside of the door, trying to catch a glimpse of the wondrous star through the door opening.

The entire group became absolutely still as the aura of the star seemed to reach out to them. Its radiance surrounded them with its light and felt to them as if they were being totally absorbed by its indescribable glow. The silence held for a long period before anyone could venture a word or even offer a thought. The beauty of the star was overwhelming and at the same time had a strange sense of beckoning, as if it would say, "Come with me".

The king was the first to move as he turned to go back into the great library room, the servants hurrying to move out of his way. One by one the seers slowly followed, each in his own world of thoughts. When the seers were all back in their places, and now sitting, the King again began to share the rest of what was on his mind.

"My heart has been having these strange feelings ever since this star appeared," he began. "I have always believed that each king may have his own star in the night sky, but this star is unlike any other star or sign I have ever seen. This star is also different and unusual in that none of you have reported seeing this star in your dominions. Tonight was the first time any of you had seen it. Why have I been able to see it clearly and you have not until tonight? I have also found that others close to my palace are not able to see this star. I believe this means that this star is a message to me about a new king who is greater, more royal, and more glorious than any other king ever known or ever to be known. Perhaps this star is the sign of the king who will be able to bring peace to all the world."

The king paused to let his words sink in and again slowly looked around the large table at each of the attentive seers. All eyes were focused on the high king, waiting eagerly for his next words.

He went on. "The reason I have summoned you is this. What I need from you, as the wisest and most knowledgeable of the seers of this kingdom, is to find out who this king is and where he is to appear. All I have in the kingdom is at your disposal! I also want you to tell me what kind of gift is suitable for me to offer to this king. For a king such as this, it must be a gift that gives honor to who he is, be personal, and also contribute to the power and glory of his kingdom.

"Please bring me your final finding as soon as you have come to a decision. I await your answer to this riddle." The king paused again in his speaking and then closed his visit with, "Honored seers, I bid you good evening and good sleep."

With that closing, the king turned and left the great library hall with all of his entourage following. The door closed on an amazed and challenged group of seers.

There was silence in that great hall for a long space while each of these men of great reputation searched their minds to see if there might be an answer buried deep in their memory. After a very long silence in which everyone seemed to wait for someone else to speak, Old One raised his head and spoke in a quiet but authoritative tone.

His eyes moving around the table, he looked at each of the seers, one at a time, a look that went deep into the heart, and then asked each one whether there was anything he could contribute to the task the king had laid before them. One after another the seers were not able to give an answer, saying that nothing in their tremendous scope of knowledge was coming to the fore that would shed a light on this deep riddle, for this question the king had presented to them was one they had never before considered. A king of the whole world was a new and strange concept. It had never been a part of common thought and was not even in their minds that it could or would ever be.

"Then," said Old One, "tomorrow we will start looking. Sleep well."

For days and even weeks they searched the library for any kind of writing that would give them a clue as to a star, or a world king to come, that they believed this sign was given to lead them to him.

One day while Agbar was seeing to his duties and the duties of the other servants, he stopped and thought of the scroll he had in his room, the only thing he had been allowed to keep when he was captured many years ago and sold into slavery. He had kept it carefully and securely in his possession for all these years. It was a writing of the prophet Isaiah, a man who had lived hundreds of years before. Agbar had been a young priest in training when his city was taken over by an invading army. He had been brought to this land and had never seen his home again.

As he thought about it, he considered how he would approach Old One, as he was a servant and there was a proto-col that must be followed.

His opportunity came very soon. On the next night, after

the seers had retired from their searching, Agbar went into the library to make sure all was in readiness for the next day. He was surprised to see several candles burning at the table. There, sitting deep in thought, was Old One, looking out the window at the night sky.

Gathering his confidence about him, for he was only a slave, Agbar, slowly with careful steps so as not to startle Old One, approached and stood quietly waiting until he was noticed. He then bowed low as the proper custom required and again waited until he was addressed by Old One.

"What is it?" came the voice of Old One. "I know you. You are called Agbar. Your service to your master is well spoken of…you may approach me at any time. What is the question you would ask at this late hour? Ask and I will attempt to give answer to you."

Agbar spoke in a voice that trembled. For a slave to speak to a person of this high authority was extremely uncommon and in some provinces would result in punishment.

He began. "Many years ago as a young man I entered a school to study the priesthood of my people who are the Hebrews. I was born of the tribe of Levi and desired to follow in the steps of this priestly tribe. It was my desire to be a priest of the God of the universe, and to this desire, I studied diligently. However, the small city I was in at the time was in the center of two warring kingdoms and I was caught in the middle of the battles, until at last one of the countries prevailed, and I with many others, were taken as slaves to the victorious army.

"The conquerors recognized that we students were not warriors, and because of that we were treated more seemly than other captives. We were told we could take one and only one personal possession with us. I chose a scroll that we as students were told by our teachers was one of the most important of all our ancient writings. This scroll was by a prophet whose name was Isaiah. He is revered by one and all of our people and his writings are kept in careful security by the priests of our God and our people.

"I have read this scroll as often as possible, but still do not understand the answers to all of the writings therein. I do remember some parts that talk about a future kingdom of peace for all.

"The reason I come to you is that I have served my master for many years, and at no time have I seen any other scrolls of my people, the Hebrews, in this room. I offer this scroll to you in hopes this prophet may perhaps offer some small insight into the answer you search for."

Old One answered Agbar in a voice that was low and gentle. "I have known your master for many years, and through him I have learned of you. I have great respect for the king, and he has spoken of you as a servant of great integrity and service; a man in whom he could place his trust. I believe you have earned the right to speak to me at any time, and with the trust your master has placed in you I can do no other. Bring me your scroll, and plan to speak with me about that which we find in it. I have actually heard of this prophet, Isaiah, but have never been able to see any of his writings, as your priests carefully kept them hidden, claiming they were only for the people of the nation for whom they were written. Bring this scroll to me. Perhaps we will both learn together."

Agbar rose from his position, and bowing low, hurried to his room, close to the king's own chambers. He quickly retrieved the Isaiah scroll from its place and carried it gingerly and protectively to the great room where he laid it on the table reverently, and very slowly and gently withdrew the cover.

"Old One," Agbar said, "here is the scroll I told you about. No one else has laid eyes on this writing other than myself since I have come to this place. It was considered a treasure by my teachers and I have kept it so."

"You have been here many years," said Old One. "Did you ever question why it was this scroll you grasped to take with you?"

"Almost never," replied Agbar. "But every time I did pick it up to read, there was a strange peace that came over me and I never got to that question. I just came to believe there was a reason I would someday learn."

"Sometimes that is all we have," said Old One. "Come, let us see what is in here. First, I want you to show me the things you remember finding, and then we will go over every word of the entire writing carefully. As I am not familiar with your people or your language, I will appreciate your help."

Carefully, they began to open the scroll and began reading, seer and servant together. When morning came, the other seers came into the room and were amazed to find the two men, seer and servant, focused on an ancient writing none had ever seen or even knew existed. The newly awakened seers gathered around as they grappled with a new writing that had never before been known to them, yet found a place in their minds. The seers were so intent on this new writing, they didn't even notice the person of the servant being in the center of activity. The new atmosphere of excitement grew as each one became involved with the new discovery being revealed for the first time. Questions were asked faster than they could be answered.

"Where was this found?"

"Where has it been?"

"Who found it?"

"Where is it from?"

"Who wrote it?"

"Was the writer a Prophet?"

"What nation was he from?"

"How old is it?"

"What is it about?"

Agbar held up his hand and when quiet fell over the group he spoke.

"Honored and wise of this land. I am a servant to your high king, but it was not always so. Many years ago I was a student preparing to be a priest of my own people, the Hebrews. Our nation was not large or powerful and so was often in the center of conflicts between the more aggressive nations which surrounded us. It was during one of these times of battles that the doors of the school of which I was a part were broken down and we faced the swords of the prevailing forces. Seeing that we put up no defense and posed no threat, they chose not to do us harm but rather to take us captive and bring us back with them where they could sell us as slaves.

"Thereupon they sheathed their weapons and bound us in

such a way that we were unable to escape, and being now prisoners of war, we were marched off to the country of the victors where we were sold as intelligent slaves to the highest bidder.

When we left in this manner, we were each allowed to take one item of choice with us. As I had just begun my study of the scroll of Isaiah, I chose to take it with me for the purpose of continuing my learning of this writing. My bidder in the slave market was of the king's personal servants from this country, and so now you see me today still in the service of your high king.

"Because I, as the personal servant to your high king, was assigned to give care to this meeting, I have been able to overhear the purpose for your search. I waited patiently to find a time that was proper for me to speak as my rank as a servant required me. Old One was gracious and allowed me to share what was on my heart about the writing in my possession. He also gave me permission to bring it to this room where he and I opened it to search its secrets. It is my belief from my teaching long ago that the text is about six or seven hundred years old, and written during a time when my whole country was in captivity in a land foreign to my people. It, with other holy writings, had been kept in the possession and care of the priests of my country's God, Jehovah, whom we believe is the great one and only God of the universe.

"It is because of our belief and trust in the great God "Jehovah" whom we worship as the creator of the whole world, that we as a people have also always been a people who look toward and believe in a future time of peace, and a leader who will bring us to that peace that is expected to be over the whole world. Our people are always unified in this desire and promise from Jehovah and have not lost the vision of that promise of the future, even when under different kingdoms.

"There were others as well in our history who wrote of this promise, but this is the only writing I have. It is now my wish to share it with you who are seekers of knowledge. It is my hope this will give more light and wisdom to your search. I will share with you those things I was taught about this scroll of Isaiah, and you through your own wisdom may find the answers you seek to this riddle which has been set before you."

Old One sat quietly for a few minutes as all the seers turned their focus on him, waiting for a word of guidance. Both Old One and Agbar had been awake all night, but with the excitement of the new scroll, neither showed the effects from lack of sleep.

Old One began. "I believe since Agbar is the only one of us who is knowledgeable in the language of this writing that Agbar should read this scroll to us and we will listen and gather our thoughts as we hear what is within its words. We will also ask questions as they come into our thinking and all may give words to the meaning that appears to us.

"Let us begin. Agbar, you will begin reading from this scroll and answer our curious natures as best as you are able."

They took their places around the large table, this time making a place for Agbar to open the scroll. As Agbar began reading in a reverent tone, he had the total attention of the seers. Even if they had not heard of Isaiah, they had heard the names of the kings named in the passage at the beginning of the scroll. Prophets were not often mentioned in the records of kingdoms but kings were almost always listed, as many times there was trade and sometimes battles between them and records were almost always kept of the treaties that were drawn between kings. The names Uzziah, Jotham, Ahaz, and Hezekiah were all names recognized by one or another of the seers.

The first passage prepared them for what they were to hear, for Agbar began reading not as the king's servant but as a high official of the king, or even a high priest. In fact, he sounded as if he were the personal herald of the great god "Jehovah" Himself. No servant ever spoke this way in the presence of the high officers. The words of the scroll overrode the thoughts of a servant speaking to high-ranking officials. In the scroll were words of condemnation, and then there were words of promise; punishment for the wrongdoers and rewards for those who did right. These were all from Jehovah and none would be able to escape.

The reading was long, as Agbar had to translate into the common language of all who listened, but the effect of the reading was the same to all who heard. There was amazement, understanding, and for some, answers as they perceived the words of a god greater than they had ever dreamed. This god, "Jehovah," spoke as if he had control over the world, men, and all things happening everywhere, and could and would reward and punish anyone he saw fit.

This was all on a personal basis that was not in the beliefs of other religions. How could a god so great care about each man or woman on an individual basis? In fact, this god talked as if he had a relationship not only with the nation but each person of that nation. This tasked the depth of understanding of the seers as they grappled with a totally new concept of thought.

As the initial reading of the scroll was completed, they sat and let their minds go over the things they had heard. No one had asked even one question as they were too absorbed in trying to take it all in.

Then, Old One broke the silence of their thoughts. "We will read this again, and then work to bring our questions to share and discuss with all. Now we need rest and nourishment."

The seers turned to their servants as food was brought to them. The meal was strangely quiet as they ate, with only a few words being spoken. These were men of much thought and knowledge, and there would be some adjusting of their understanding to add the new information to what they already had. Finally they separated for the evening, each to his own room to ponder what they had heard and create the questions they would ask the next day.

They came into the great library the next morning and at the suggestion of several of them, they decided to have Agbar read the scroll again. This was the same for three days.

On the fourth day, at the end of the reading of the scroll, Old One stood to his feet and said, "Who is this Jehovah? I have heard of many gods with many names but never one who spoke like this. This God called "Jehovah" claims the whole world as his dominion, manages kings and governments and even things that happen to the nature around us. He punishes the evildoer and promises rewards to the good. He even says what is good and evil in his sight. He speaks to his people by name, something no other god that I know of has ever done. He promises peace to his people and the whole world and is sending the leader of that peace, the "King of Peace."

"This god tells his people exactly what he plans to do before it is done.

"I ask all of you to search to the deepest part of your knowledge to see if you have anything to compare with our findings in this writing. We will meet two days hence to compare any information you may have found with our thoughts and our questions. I bid you good evening and good slumber."

These great wise men turned to taking in the food which was prepared for them. Conversation this late afternoon was characterized by scholarly discussion and respectful challenges as every belief that was known to many was brought forth and fathomed for its true meaning.

After two days of this kind of total consuming thought and comparison discussion, all began to realize that the God "Jehovah" was the only entity who could be the key to the puzzle of the star.

Agbar was an important part of these conversations as he explained the history of the Hebrew nation, which all Hebrews committed to memory from a very young age. At last, one by one they began to come to the end of the journey through the deepest store rooms of their minds, and came to sit at the large table again, resting in the satisfaction they had come to the answer they were seeking.

Old One was already at the table watching as each man took his seat. When they were all there at last in their places, he asked, "Have you an answer?"

Almost as one they came back with their reply. "We have an answer. Jehovah is indeed the God who must be given praise for this sign in the night sky."

"Then, we are as one," said Old One, adding his confirmation to the rest. "Now, what gifts should we choose?" was the next question from Old One.

"Gold," came the first answer, "for to begin and build a kingdom, all kings need gold. This gift is one especially for royalty." The gift of gold met with unanimous agreement.

"There must be a gift to bring one into personal favor with the new king. I would think Myrrh, a most fragrant and personal gift of great value." This from a seer called "Longbeard" for the great, long, flowing growth of hair upon his chin, a fact that he was not unproud of. "Myrrh is the most sought after of all personal accents."

Within the private circle of these high king's advisors there was not only a close comradery, but use of short names given as to close friends. These names were unknown outside of this circle of men, but they enjoyed the ability to converse without using their long and courtly titles each time they spoke to one another. This also made the sharing of information and the discussion easier. It was only a very short discussion to make this another gift of unified agreement.

"I would offer frankincense." The voice came from a short seer whose age had rendered him stooped over and walking with the aid of a cane. His name in this group was "Threelegs", and his voice was thin and high-pitched and crackled when he spoke, but because of his age and his place as second only to Old One in knowledge, no one took notice of the unusual quality or the sound of his voice, or his cane. "I believe that this "Jehovah" desires praise and worship from his subjects. Frankincense is the fragrance most used for worship in the temples of our kingdoms and I suggest that it would be pleasing when worship was given by this new and highest of kings to his god. It would most assuredly bring this new king into Jehovah's favor."

"That is an excellent choice," said Greentop, a name given because of his luminous green head covering. "If this king of the future is indeed who we believe he is, he will need and want the favor of Jehovah."

After a very short time of talking about the three gifts, they were all agreed that the choices were good ones.

"Have we fulfilled the requests of the king?" asked Old One. This brought a moment of silence as each seer remembered and reviewed the request the king had put before them.

"I believe it is time to call the king and give him the information we have found," said Old One. He turned to Agbar. "It is time. Go and inform your master that we have an answer for him."

The king arrived in a short time, having been anxiously awaiting the finding of the seers.

After listening carefully and giving consideration to the ideas given to him from Old One, speaking for the whole group, he then again astonished the meeting by saying, "I would ask that this group be my representatives to this new and high king."

The seers gaped at the king as his request froze them in place. "Oh, king," Greentop spoke. "It is a long journey to this land in which this chosen child is to be born. It will be dangerous and require many weeks of travel and great planning." Greentop was one of great wisdom, and also great worry. If there was nothing available to worry about, Greentop would have a list.

"Part of this planning has already been done," said the king, "as Agbar has been keeping me aware of your work, he also told me that he was very sure you would find the king in his home country of Israel. He was so sure of that he asked me for permission to have plans started for a caravan to travel and visit this new king. As I have come to trust Agbar with many things during his service to me, even my life, I have given him permission to have the work begun. You will find the preparations for your journey even now in progress. Please have your personal servants give to Agbar the personal needs required for each of you. I hope to see you on your way thirty days hence. There is also a valiant group of warriors who will go with you as guards for your safety. They have been carefully chosen for their valor. The leader for this journey is an experienced soldier called "Ment." You may trust him and all of them with your very lives."

As the high king turned to leave, he stopped and turned back to the still-in-shock seers and said, "May the great God "Jehovah" of the Hebrews watch over you and shower his blessings upon you and your journey." He then turned away to the door and left.

There was nothing left to say. Old One looked over his group—now travel companions—and said, "Make careful preparations. This may be the most important journey we will ever make."

With nods and murmurs of assent, the seers gathered their servants and left the great library to begin preparing for a visit to the "King of Peace" as he was now called by all of them.

The next few days were filled with a flurry of activity as fourteen different sets of servants made ready for the same journey. Add to that the soldiers and animal caretakers, all trying to work together and yet doing different things with the same purpose. The seers would be riding camels, while the soldiers would be on horses. The servants would be walking and herding the spare animals.

Ment was everywhere, organizing and seeing that the proper order was being established. The supplies were to be carried on smaller pack animals and each kind of animal had a different diet which had to be prepared for. The total number of animals and people numbered in the hundreds and Ment turned out to be a master at organization. In twenty-six days the entire company was ready and the order was given to move early in the morning of the twenty-seventh day.

Agbar was given a special place in the caravan close to the front with Ment and the seers. The king himself ordered that Agbar ride atop a horse like Ment was riding.

On the morning of the twentieth day, the king called for Agbar to meet with him for a report on the preparations. As Agbar gave his report, the king could see the excitement of his faithful servant when he spoke of once again seeing the homeland he had left so many years ago.

At the end of the report, the king looked at Agbar and then spoke in a warm and gentle tone.

"You are going home. I will miss you when you are gone. I do not have the thanks you have earned while here in the service of my home and my kingdom. You have never complained, but have done everything in your power to give service to me. You have treated me not as your master but as your father. It is for all of this that I am giving Old One a letter granting your freedom and permission to leave the caravan and once again stay in your homeland to live out your days in peace under the worship of your god. I grant you this in gratefulness, for I have also come to think of you as my son. Go in peace and may Jehovah, your God, bless you all the days of your life."

At the king's words, Agbar went to his knees and put his face on the floor as tears rolled down his face. He could barely get the words out as he said, "O King and my Master. I too am filled with sadness as well as joy; for you, O King, have never mistreated me but given me care and respect I never expected to receive as one in this position. You have granted me trust and honor and I have grown to love you as my father. I will also miss you, for I know no other life than that which I have lived here in this kingdom. I will pray to Jehovah that he also will pour abundant blessings on you and your house forever. May your kingdom be peaceful for your life and your sons after you."

King and slave embraced for a long moment, and Agbar turned and left his master to go to the caravan and finish the few things needed to leave.

On the final morning, Ment—dressed in such a way to announce his place as the leader—gave the order to march, and all the sleepy men and animals started heading out in the planned order which was absolutely necessary for a caravan of this size. Ment led the way on a prancing stallion and right beside and slightly behind rode the standard bearer holding the king's flag proudly waving in the morning breeze.

There were many people out to see them off, waving scarves to all in the large column.

It took only a few days for the company to fall into a regular and consistent order. The day's work started every morning before daylight while it was yet cool, getting both people and animals moving around and the morning meal served. There were tents to take down and pack, and all animals were thoroughly looked over to make sure there were no pack irritations, for that would cause a problem later.

Ment was always up ahead of everyone else and seemed to be everywhere at once, encouraging, advising and hurrying the process as though the time was exceedingly short.

The caravan had been traveling thirteen weeks when Ment spoke to Agbar and said, "We are close to the edge of the Roman empire. Please be alert for my call as I may ask for your assistance with language."

Agbar nodded and also became watchful as the word went out to the other members of the guards and to the rest of the caravan to be alert to the presence of strangers approaching, including soldiers.

It was only two days later they were approached by a patrol of Roman soldiers on horseback. Ment went ahead to meet with the leader of this group and they talked briefly, while the caravan stopped and waited. Finally, Ment raised a hand as the two leaders turned and went on their different ways and the signal was given to again move out.

After they were moving again, Ment rode over to Agbar and Old One and told them what had transpired in the conversations. Ment told them the centurion had indeed inquired as to why they were traveling so heavily guarded in this direction, toward the center of the empire.

"When I told them we were on our way to see the king with gifts and were not here for battle, he gave us permission to go, but with a warning, and also that there would be taxes collected at numerous points along the way. He did not mention or know of a new king who had been born. He did remember there was an area called Judea in the country to the west toward the sea but had never been there himself. We separated as two non-warring soldiers normally would and we are now able to move on." When they started moving again, the star was as always before them.

After the meeting with the Roman soldiers, there arose some doubts among the servants as many of them were not trained in battle and they were afraid they would be called upon to fight.

This rumor brought up the question of whether they were going in the correct direction. Agbar and Old One conferred and Old One asked if it were possible for Jehovah God to show also the star to the others.

Agbar thought and then said that he would make this request of Jehovah. He did. That night, after camp was set, all three leaders stood up before the gathered members of travelers and Old One said, "We have heard that there are doubts among you as to our purpose and direction. Our purpose is to honor a new king above all kings. Our direction is guided by his star."

As he spoke, he pointed in the direction they had been traveling and the star was there, evident for all to look upon. The whole company of servants gasped as what they had only heard rumors about was before them in that same beauteous glow for all to see. From that time on there was a new sense about the work as everyone now had seen the same guide that had brought them this far. The caravan seemed to travel farther each day and with less problems from the animals as if they also now sensed the common purpose of their journey.

After more weeks of changing lands from desert to green valleys and back again, the caravan approached a river that caused the heart of Agbar to suddenly beat like a hammer. He rode ahead to Ment, and moving up beside the soldier, he said, "I know this place. Please allow me a few moments now to dismount."

Ment stopped, and as he did so, Agbar jumped down from the horse he was riding. Running forward to the side of the river, he bent down and placed his face to the ground and kissed it.

"This is my homeland. I am home!" He shouted and danced and leaped around to the confusion of those who did not know what was happening.

As it was already later in the day, Ment called the order to camp and requested Agbar and the seers to meet with him after they had eaten. After all were seated, Ment looked at Agbar and said, "Tell me all you can remember about this place and this land that I may be properly knowledgeable as we come closer to our destination."

Agbar began sharing from his memory of the days when he was a youth and the things he could recall about his home country from the time of his studies for the priesthood. After he had run out of words and breath, Ment turned toward Old

One and they began deciding about how to go through this land in a manner that would be conducive to finding the child.

After a brief period, it was the conclusion that they should go the present ruler of the area to which they were going and present themselves. Agbar had shared with the leaders everything he knew about the town, Bethlehem, mentioned in another prophet's writing. The prophet's name was Micah, but Agbar could only remember the name of the town and that it was both the birthplace of King David and it was close to Jerusalem. Jerusalem was the capital of Israel located in the region called Judah.

With the decision made to start at Jerusalem, they began preparing for what they hoped was the last stage of their journey. As before, when they turned to the south toward Judah and Jerusalem, the star was before them.

The caravan, now sensing that they were close to their goal, moved along in almost a jovial mood. Several days later they came in sight of Jerusalem. Nothing they had heard or been told prepared them for the vision that was now before them. The temple mount with its glowing beauty on the high hill; the Antonia fortress, a massive building structure; and the entire city presented them with a breathtaking view.

Pausing only for a moment, Ment found a place not far from the city where they could camp for the night and they set up for the evening. Ment, with Old One, Greentop, Threelegs, and Agbar, began working on their plans for the visit to the palace and the audience with the king, Herod.

The next morning the five representatives set out to the palace, having sent messengers before them with a gift to prepare the way. They were inspected carefully by everyone in the narrow, winding streets until they came to the palace itself. There, they were received with the standard ceremony of a monarch. After many formalities, the king asked "What is your mission in this land?"

The answer was not what he had expected to hear.

"We have come seeking the King of Peace, spoken of in the old writings. Can you direct us to where he may be found? We have seen his sign, a great star in the sky, and have come to pay him homage."

"What is this king of peace?" the king asked. "For I know of no writing that speaks of one to come."

"We have found this in in the writings of a prophet named Isaiah," they answered.

"I have heard of this prophet but not of this king." Herod paused for a moment. "I will ask of the priests of the temple," he said, and immediately called one of the attendants standing close. "Go and call to me the high priest and some of the elders of the temple. I want to inquire of those who know of the prophets."

Herod then had his servants take the group from the caravan to another room where they were served food and asked to wait for a call from the king.

In a short time there appeared in the hearing room the chief priest and several elders just as the king had requested. They had already been forewarned of the king's question and were prepared to give an answer, for they had for many years discussed the coming of one called "Messiah", but were afraid to mention it in front of a ruler who tolerated none other than himself in power.

"Oh king," they began, carefully thinking out words that would not irritate this monarch.

"There is one mentioned in the old prophets, but we do not believe that now is the time, or that he is to come against you. You are the sole king over this land." This was said to belay the king from checking too close and to send him down another pathway of thoughts. This group of priests and elders were very careful to protect their own standing under this monarch.

The king stroked his beard for a moment, gave the priest and elders a careful look and then asked, "Who is this king? Where is this king to rule? Where is he to be born, or has he now been born? How are we to know this king? What is his name?"

The high priest had no choice but to tell the king what the prophets had said. When he heard the name Bethlehem, the king's eyes seemed to narrow slightly, and he again stroked his beard as he contemplated what he had just been told. Seeming to come to a decision, he arose from his ruling seat and ordered his aide to bring the seers again into his presence.

All the way through this exchange the group from the caravan were waiting in a room down a hallway far enough away such that they were not able to hear the exchange between the king and the high priest. While waiting, little conversation was attempted, for all of them had the same feeling of evil and foreboding that seemed to surround this king, Herod.

When they were called back into the king's presence, they were not ready for the answer that was given to them. They were instructed to go and find the new king and then return with the information as to where he could be found because this king also wanted to go and pay proper homage to him.

Thanking the king, the group left the palace as quickly as they could, and went straight to their encampment to share the news with the other seers and prepare for the short journey as they had been told it was only a short distance to the town of Bethlehem. They did not speak of their experience at the palace to all, only to the other seers, for there was a feeling of unease and the need to leave right away.

As soon as the order was given to move, the leaders looked up and the star was again there before them, leading them onward. Its presence was comforting, for they knew they were very close, even though the feeling they sensed from Herod had not entirely gone away. The star was telling them to continue on.

The distance to the small town of Bethlehem was indeed short, and the town of such small size, that the huge caravan stopped a short distance away from the town. As it was past the noon time, they set up camp. The people in the town watched with wondering eyes as the size and number of members in this particular group was greater than had ever stopped at this small town.

Two of the members of the caravan stepped away from the work of setting up camp, and mounting their horses, rode toward the center of the town. While the first was dressed in the normal dress of the lands in this part of the world, the other was dressed as a high-ranking soldier, with weapons hanging from belts and girdles wrapped around about his torso. A massive sword was the first thing to see but there were knives in several places with blades both curved and straight. The first one turned and spoke to Caleb who was standing in front of all the others trying to get the best position to see everything. The voice was gentle and the language was their own. The question was simple. "Where is the inn?"

Caleb, who was totally overwhelmed by what he was seeing and what was happening in his small town, could not speak but only pointed to the building where the innkeeper was also watching. If anything was happening in Bethlehem, the innkeeper would know, for all news seemed to flow through his location and business, and the town was packed with people.

The two men had a brief conversation with the innkeeper, and then remounted and rode back to the large encampment, starting a mad rush to the innkeeper's door as everyone in town wanted to know what was said and who these men were. The innkeeper waited until the noise and talking had subsided enough to be heard, and then told the people that the two men had asked about a child born in this town, and gave the time of birth.

This caused many more questions that the innkeeper could not answer. At the innkeeper's unsatisfactory response to the crowd's questions, there was a short pause while the crowd thought up and considered their next inquiries.

"What child?"

"How did they know a child had been born here?"

"How did they know when the child was born?"

"Where were they from?"

"Why did they want to know about this child?"

"Why were they here?"

"Why was this child so important to them to have traveled so far?"

"How long did they travel?"

"Why so many people in one caravan?

"Why were the camels dressed so ornately?"

"Why were there so many soldiers? They were not dressed like Roman soldiers. What army were they part of?"

At last the innkeeper held up his hands. "I do not know the answers to your questions," he said. "Just wait and watch as I will do and then perhaps we can learn more."

This pacified the crowd for the moment and they started to move away towards their homes, all the time looking toward the large camp outside the city as they walked, and each one listing in their minds the possible reasons for the strangers stopping here. This was not the normal stopping point for large caravans.

It was not long before there was a new and different kind of event to draw the attention from the townspeople, as from the direction of the caravan camp came a unique group dressed in garments of fine cloth of many bright colors, adorned with silk sashes, also of bright hues.

There were also on their heads turbans of amazing styles, also in bright colors. They came quietly with little or no conversation, and moved directly as with a great purpose to the lodging that had come to be known as the carpenter's house. This was the house that the young tax collector had brought the baby's family to from the stable. They had remained there since the birth of their child in the stable and had fit in nicely with other families in neighboring homes.

Many homes in this land were built in a set of three around a small common area where there was a single fire and oven for bread making. Most often these were the homes of relatives. The one home in this trio was the home that had been left to the young tax collector at the death of his parents. A relative and his family lived in the second dwelling. The third was the carpenter's.

The gate of the common area opened to the center street of the town and it was to this gate that the seers, followed by their servants, went. Agbar went to the gate to the common area and called to the occupants.

Two women came to the gate. One was older, of middle age. The other was young and followed by a little boy holding to his mother's hand, as he too wanted to see the owner of the strange voice at the entrance to their home.

Agbar spoke gently as Ment was still beside him in full soldier dress and may have alarmed the women. "Do not be alarmed," he said. "We have come a far distance seeking the child born to be the King of Peace."

The mother's heart leapt within her as she remembered again the angel's words that had been spoken to her that night.

Agbar continued, "We have come a great distance following a star that was sent to guide us, and it has at long last led us to this place. Is the child here? We have come to give him honor."

The young woman looked from Agbar to the small child and said, "This is the child you seek, as it was foretold to me by an angel that he would someday be king."

Agbar bowed low to the child who was still in wonder, holding to his mother's hand. He arose, turned to Ment and said, "It is time to bring the others."

Ment went to the gate and beckoned to the seers who came,

looked in, and then began filling the space in the common cooking area, which was not expecting a crowd of fourteen at one time.

The servants of the seers, as each of the seers had several, were left outside the common area, ready to do any bidding of their masters.

The mother stood unable to speak as she looked at the beautiful colors of the clothing, the head coverings, and the decorative scarves, each trying to be more colorful than the others.

When all were within the common courtyard, there was a short moment of silence as every seer gazed upon the boy who was in turn busy looking around at the great number of strange visitors who crowded into his home.

Then Old One went to his knees, bowed low to the ground, and in his own language, greeted and spoke homage to the new king. Each of the seers also bowed and followed the lead of Old One, and for a moment, the sound of many languages spoken in unison but with different words gave forth a sound like waves on a seashore.

This for the toddler was above his level of understanding. While all the seers were bowed with their faces to the ground, he ventured forward, fascinated by the colors in the head attire of Old One, as he was the closest. Then in a moment of impulse, the toddler reached out and pulled the turban-style headdress from the head of Old One and put it on his own head where—being much too large for the boy's head—it slipped down over one eye, where it sat at an angle and covered it.

Old One raised his head and looked at the boy who looked back at Old One with one eye and grinned and giggled.

There was a communal gasp as the others saw a never before seen view of the bald and shining dome of Old One's head, and his personal covering on top of a toddler. There was an absolute silence as every seer held his breath, afraid to speak or even move.

Then came a sound they had never before heard from the aged leader. It started as a small chuckle, and then started growing into a laughter that grew stronger the longer it went.

Now the child joined in and as it went on, the infectious sound engulfed every one of the seers and even the mother and the other woman of the house. As the laughter grew, the boy began yelling louder and showing off his new head covering until it seemed the whole town of Bethlehem had to hear.

When it began finally to subside, Old One held out his arms to the toddler who ran to him and allowed himself to be swept into the arms of Old One, and wrapping his small arms around the neck of Old One, the two hugged furiously as old friends long separated.

This activity and sounds of joy had summoned the man of the house and he stopped just inside the doorway with a look of wonder at the sight in front of him. His carpentry tools were still in his hands as he looked around at what was usually a quiet home, but was now stuffed with men he did not know, but who were dressed as royalty and were rocking with mirth. His little boy was in the arms of one of these strangers and was wearing the turban of the one who was holding him.

Agbar had no need to translate the laughter but was ready when Old One turned to the mother and asked, "What name has been given to this child?"

The mother answered Agbar's question with the words, "He is called "Jesus" for this is the name the angel gave us."

Old One listened to Agbar's translation, then whispered the name quietly to himself, and as all looked on, he held the toddler high in his arms for all to see and spoke to all who were there with the caravan. "This is the King of the World. His name is Jesus. He is the true King of Peace."

Again there were voices raised in many languages giving praise to the new king. The seers gave praise in their personal language. There was then a second showering of praise in the common language of the combined kingdom which Agbar translated for the parents and the others listening just outside the gate.

After a long time of praise, the level of sound began to decrease and the thoughts of proper hospitality began to arise in the minds of the women of the town who were outside the gate looking over the short wall at the front of the enclosure. Someone voiced the thought of the home having more guests than they would be able to feed and the word spread immediately to the women of the town to bring bread, figs, and other foods to serve.

As it was just past baking time, there was an abundance of food gathered for the guests, and quickly a meal sat before them. As this visit was for the young child, the ladies of the town took over the duties of serving the food and would not let the mother help but insisted that she sit with her son and husband.

While the meal was being prepared, Old One spoke again. "We would hear of how this came about from the very beginning. Please do not leave anything out, for we are seekers of the truth."

The young mother looked at her husband for confirmation and then began speaking, Agbar translating to the guests from the caravan.

"I was asleep on my mat when I was awakened by a strange light which shone brightly around me. As I looked, I saw this being I can only believe was an angel, who spoke to me. He greeted me and told me I should not fear, for Jehovah had looked upon me with favor. He then said that I would have a baby boy and should call his name Jesus.

"The angel also said that Jehovah would give him the throne of David and He would reign over the house of Jacob forever. I asked the angel how could this be as I was yet a single maiden and knew not a man. The angel told me that I would be pregnant by the Holy Ghost and the child would be called the Son of God.

"My mother sent me to visit a cousin by the name of Elizabeth, for she was also with child at a very old age, and her husband was a priest of great respect. When I greeted her at her door, the baby in her womb seemed to dance with joy.

"I returned to my home where my father had to speak to my husband. In our country, when a couple becomes engaged, they are considered as husband and wife, even though the marriage is not yet consummated. The penalty for adultery is extremely severe, even stoning. My husband was also visited by an angel who told him he was to take me home immediately as his wife.

"He rose from his bed and came to my father's house in the

third watch of the night and took me to his home. Then the census came and we had to go to the city of our fathers to be counted, so you see me here with my husband and this boy whom Jehovah has given us.

"The night he was born we found lodging only in the stable of the inn. We then came to this house where my husband has found work as a carpenter. Here you find us still."

The food was served and conversation continued with many questions and comments.

Agbar was translating as fast as he could and barely had a moment to eat and relax.

At last Old One felt it was time to close the gathering down. He stood and said, "We also have gifts for this young king." He signaled to his servant to have the gifts brought in that had been decided upon by the seers long ago in the planning meeting.

The servants were ready and came through the gateway bearing three boxes, one much heavier than the other two.

Old One now turned to the parents who were sitting together holding the young boy. "These gifts we bring to honor this new king," he began. "May he reign forever in glory, majesty, and peace. May the God of all the world bless his kingdom above all others that have ever been or ever shall be."

Old One signaled the servant with the heavy box to come forward first and place the box before the boy who was now sitting with his parents. "We bring this young king gold for the establishment of his kingdom."

The next servant stepped forward and placed his box beside the first. "We bring him frankincense for the moments of offering and sacrifice to his God."

The last of three servants came to add his box to the others. "We bring him myrrh for personal times of worship."

"May these gifts be accepted with the love with which they are given," Old One concluded with a very low bow.

The couple sat quiet, overwhelmed by what was happening and being said about and around them and their young son.

Old One, always being perceptive, then went on. "The time for our purpose in coming is over. Come let us be joyful, for the goal of our journey has been fulfilled."

A period of fellowship followed as people of different languages worked to communicate, which brought spells of confusion and laughter. The child they had come so far to meet had returned Old One's turban and was now going from one to another of the seers, giving them hugs and laughing at them and with them. It was a time of gentleness and peace; even the others in this small crowded town were stopping by to meet these great visitors.

But it also came time for the seers to depart this gathering, and bidding the proper goodbye to all, the seers left the small family and made their way to the large campground they had occupied. They began to prepare for a night of sleep knowing they were not done but had a long trip to their home.

It was past the middle of the night when Old One sat suddenly upright from his mat. He looked around to see the other seers doing the same. Looking at each other there was a look of consternation on their faces; then a look of surprise as they saw that all were awake at the same time. No one spoke for a time, waiting for someone else to start the words that were difficult to speak.

Finally, Old One asked the closest to him. "Did you also dream?"

The next seer answered, "I did. And it was a warning to leave and go a different way to our home for the safety and well-being of all our people."

Just at that time, Threelegs came to where they were sitting, now fully awake. "My brothers, we must be on our way immediately. I do not know the reason why, but I was warned in a dream to rise and go as soon as we can get under way."

By this time the other seers were joining them and every one had received the same warning to leave as soon as possible.

Old One rose from his position and called his chief servant. "Bring Ment to me now."

The chief servant had never been spoken to in that way and left at a hard run to where Ment had been seen lying down. He returned with Ment running right beside him.

Old One looked at Ment and said, "Prepare us to depart at once and plan another route home far different than the way we came."

Ment took one look at the entire group of seers and said, "At once," and was gone to rouse the camp. In a very short time the feeling of urgency was upon all of the members of the caravan and they began moving out in a very quiet manner so as not to alarm the townspeople. Soon they were out of sight, leaving only marks of the large group who had been here.

The only one to see them go was an old trader who was also leaving on his way to Egypt. He was already behind schedule because of a lame pack animal. The animal was again able to travel and this merchant was now trying to make up for lost time by traveling in the early morning hours. This was only a very short time behind the leaving of the huge caravan that had started to move away from the town, when there suddenly appeared beside him a young man.

Startled, the trader stopped what he was doing as the young man came close and said in a low voice, "I was told you are going to Egypt. We would ask that you let us go with you. We will not hold you up and will do our part as we travel. It is just I, my wife, and a young son who will not be a burden, as I will carry him whenever needed, to keep up. We are ready at this moment to leave."

The trader had never had a request like this before, but the man looked in good health and he could always use help feeding the animals, and they were also ready to leave.

Soon, the night was again quiet around this small town of Bethlehem.

THE STORY AS TOLD FROM THE BIBLE
IN THE BOOK OF MATTHEW
MATTHEW CHAPTER 2 VERSES 1-14 (ESV)

Now after Jesus was born in Bethlehem of Judea in the days of Herod the king, behold, wise men from the east came to Jerusalem, saying, "Where is he who has been born king of the Jews? For we saw his star when it rose and have come to worship him. When Herod the king heard this, he was troubled, and all Jerusalem with him; and assembling all the chief priests and scribes of the people, he inquired of them where the Christ was to be born.

They told him, "In Bethlehem of Judea, for it is so written by the prophets.

'And you, O Bethlehem, in the land of Judah
Are by no means least among the rulers of Judah,
For from you shall come a ruler
Who will shepherd my people Israel.'

Then Herod summoned the wise men secretly and ascertained from them what time the star had appeared. And he sent them to Bethlehem, saying, "Go and search diligently for the child. And when you have found him, bring me word, that I too may come and worship him."

After listening to the king, they went on their way. And, behold, the star that they had seen when it rose went before them until it came to rest over the place where the child was. When they saw the star, they rejoiced exceedingly with great joy.

And going into the house, they saw the child with Mary his mother, and they fell down and worshiped him. Then, opening their treasures, they offered him gifts, gold and frankincense and myrrh. And being warned in a dream not to return to Herod, they departed to their own country by another way.

Now when they had departed, an angel appeared to Joseph in a dream and said, "Rise, take the child and his mother and flee to Egypt, and remain there until I tell you, for Herod is about to search for the child, to destroy him." And he rose and took the child and his mother and departed to Egypt, and remained there until the death of Herod.

The Long Ride Home

It was late evening. The sun was setting low in the west over the great sea, almost as low as the feeling in the heart of the centurion as he rode to the small town where he had a house to come to for a rare time away from Jerusalem.

Bethlehem, a small town, busy with the many travelers and visitors for the census, normal except for that one night. That night came easily back into focus in his mind as he remembered all the events that happened, all in one night. So many things, all seemingly connected to the baby born in the stable of the inn.

Even the king's order to kill all boys under two seemed to be related to that one night almost two years ago. It was all in this horrible picture. Just why the birth of one tiny boy could cause so much tragedy was beyond the understanding of this centurion. He had never been able to remove this baby from his thoughts. In fact, he had seen the boy with his mother often when in Bethlehem and following in the shadow of the husband as the man worked at his skill of carpentry. The little boy would pick up one tool after another and imitate using them as he had watched the actions of the carpenter.

The town that night of his birth had been crammed tight with all who claimed to be in the lineage of David, an ancient King. That was the way people were counted, according to the family from which they were descended.

So many people had come to Bethlehem. It was a wonder the roofs didn't all fall in from the visitors and family members sleeping up there. The walls of the houses absolutely were ready to crumble under the extra weight. In fact, the town was going to be this crowded for a long time as the census would continue until the Romans were satisfied with the final reports.

Jewish hospitality required that everyone host as many as possible who came to their city, but there were only so many houses, and definitely not enough for the huge number who had come for this crazy census. Even if the government wanted more money, this was a strange way of getting it done, but the people of this country did place enormous emphasis on family lineage. Who you were was totally dependent on which family tree you were part of.

Bethlehem was the center of that thought as this was the birthplace of the ancient king named David. For some reason, that particular king and his line of descendants was the most important line to the people of the whole nation.

He wondered how the young couple who had come in so late were related to the line of this king, David. Whatever the connection, the husband of the young couple had actually taken the journey with his young wife, ready to give birth, but then had ended up in the stable of the inn. Apparently, there were no relatives here with a place for them.

The baby had arrived. Then, for some reason, a group of shepherds came running in from the hills outside of town, leaving their sheep, to see the baby. But then these same shepherds left to go back to the fields, shouting something about a Messiah.

He had asked the Rabbi about this "Messiah" and learned why the town could be so excited. This town was where the Hebrew prophets had predicted the Jewish Messiah would be born. If this was their promised Messiah the Hebrews had been expecting for a thousand years, they were going to be ecstatic and the Roman government was going to have more problems than they already had.

He had never heard of a king being born in a stable. What kind of a king was that? Most royalty was born in a palace or the home of some very important person. There should also be many important government officials present. This birth was so abnormal.

He had hired the father of the baby to do some work for his house while he went to see his son in Nazareth and the work was extremely well done. He had also watched this family as the baby had begun to grow as a child. In fact, the young tax collector had let them live in one of his houses. They were still there. That was all almost two years ago.

And now, this. How was this birth that happened in the stable that night connected to the order from the king? What was the purpose? Why would you kill innocent children this young? What harm could a child of two cause to a kingdom, especially the Roman Empire?

The heart of the centurion trembled with grief. He had ordered soldiers unfamiliar with the town of Bethlehem to perform the duty so they would not have to act against those they may have known personally. He knew his men. He would probably have to deal with a morale problem over this. His men were strict but not overly so. The children here did not fear the soldiers as they did in many parts of the empire.

As he rode the trail toward the little town he could feel the pain, the anger, and the sorrow of those he passed on the way. How was he to face the people he had come to know and actually become friends with, especially the parents of that little boy?

As he neared the town, he found he had to fight back tears. This was not good. It was not seemly that he, a centurion, would ever shed a tear over doing his job and even worse if he seemed sympathetic to the subject peoples he was to oversee.

He went to his house and called his aide who had been in charge while he remained in Jerusalem. He asked the aide how the people were handling the "purge" as it was called.

"Tears, grief, anger. I would expect nothing else," said the aide.

"And the family of the carpenter?" the centurion asked carefully.

"They are gone," came the return.

"Gone!" The centurion looked at his aide in surprise.

"Yes, gone in the night, the same night right after a caravan with some high officials left".

"What caravan?" The centurion was amazed. Large caravans did not normally stop in this small town, especially if there were high officials traveling with it. Traders in groups sometimes stopped for a night but an official caravan was normally quite large and would go to a large city for night stops.

"From where? Why? How large? Where were they going?" asked the centurion.

The aide's answer came carefully and thoughtfully. "They came from somewhere in the east. I don't know where or why, but it was very large. Over 250 animals, camels and supply animals. The men riding the camels were in fine gold with many servants chasing around, and a large group of guards, with permission to travel here, of course. The caravan was greater in size than this town. The amazing thing was that the leaders, those that wore clothing trimmed in gold, stopped at the house of the carpenter. After a while they went back to camp, but they were gone in the morning. They packed up suddenly in the night and left in a hurry."

The centurion sat back in his chair. He was happy about the little family avoiding the death order, but curious about the behavior of the caravan. What could this all mean? And was this the same caravan that had caused such a stir in Jerusalem while he was there? This is all connected somehow.

He turned to the work that was waiting for him on his table

The Runaway Seer

Looking over one's shoulder for more than a glance was always difficult from the seat high on the back of a camel. But once again as he had already done a thousand times in the last several days, Greentop stared back at where they had been, searching for any dark speck or wisp of dust that would indicate that they were being followed. Seeing nothing, he turned with a sigh back to urge the great gangly beast to a greater speed, (as if one ever could convince a camel to hurry when it was not in the mood and tired).

He had known from the beginning that this trip was ill fated. He had tried to tell the others in the caravan that there would be trouble. Of course they would not listen.

There had been a great period of time, study, and failure to find what they were seeking, and then, only when the servant of the high king had brought a scroll from a people who guarded their beliefs with a passion and kept their scrolls secreted away, did they find what seemed to be the answer. There were still questions, but what they found in the writings of the Hebrew prophet Isaiah was the only thing that fit the missing piece to the puzzle in their minds.

Between the study of the ancient writings and the couriers riding to the different kingdoms for supplies and other travel needs including food for man and animals, the study to find the answer and the preparation for the journey had taken almost two entire seasons. Then they had traveled for almost two seasons more toward an unknown location in Palestine.

The caravan was larger than any of its members had ever been part of before, and they had only a vague idea of the distance they would have to actually travel. They knew only that the star remained ever before them, moving as they moved, keeping just ahead so as to be seen, and giving them a good direction. Somewhere in the land of the Hebrews they would find the true king, the one of the ancient prophesies, he that was destined to rule the world in peace. He would be in Bethlehem.

The caravan was extremely large because of its mission, consisting of over 250 animals and over 180 men, including 14 seers, animal keepers, servants, and a large number of guards. Yet with all this there were only three gifts that were deemed suitable for the king found in the prophetic writings; gold which is always needed by a king, and two fragrances, one for the personal living and one for worship and sacrifice. These gifts were by agreement of all fourteen seers.

All of these fourteen seers had been hand chosen by their respective kings or rulers as the highest representative of their kingdoms.

The trip had been a long one culminating in the city of Jerusalem, the capital of the land to which the prophesies had pointed. It was anticipated that the country would be in celebration about the birth of the "Anointed One", and for this reason, the caravan naturally went to the center of government in order to pay homage.

What the seers did not expect was the reception they received, not only from the ruling Romans, but also from the Jewish leaders as well. First, there was a seemingly total ignorance of any such event taking place. Second, there was a noticeable feeling of resentment from both Romans and Jews at the mention of a king who would be a ruler of the world. Both groups indeed seemed to want to know little about the prophesies.

Herod, the Roman appointed king, seemed deceptive when he offered to help find where the new king would be born. In fact, just the way he acted made a man look over his shoulder when he was leaving. There was just something mean and vile about him that spoke of an evil within.

Herod's request made of the seers to return with the location of the new king did not line up with the attitudes and actions that should be present with a new king's arrival.

The seers were quite nervous. But when they did leave Jerusalem, the star appeared again in front of them and once again led them onward.

They were led to the small town of Bethlehem and there paid the proper homage to the child. The gifts were presented as planned and then something happened that had all of them rattled. That night after finding the child, the seers were awakened by a dream in the middle of the night. Each of the seers had the same dream. It came in the form of a warning to leave and get out of the country and away from Herod as soon as possible.

They immediately awakened the entire caravan and left in the night by a different direction.

The caravan was ordered to move with all haste with only stops to feed and water the animals for the first two days. They expected at any time to see a cloud of dust behind them from a Roman legion chasing them.

That was five days ago, and most of them had started to worry less about being followed.

Threelegs was also worried, but even as he worried about his own safety, other thoughts kept coming into his mind and would not leave.

What was so special about this child? What would Herod do about him? What would the religious leaders do? Who would keep him safe? Where could he go to grow up in safety? What god would he serve? Who would crown him? What would his kingdom be like?

How long would his kingdom last?

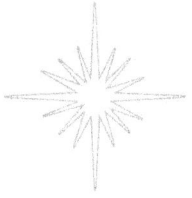

Home at Last

The king sat impatiently waiting for the report from Old One and the seers. They had just arrived back from their journey after many months.

The door to the throne room opened and the king stared in surprise as the first person in the door was not Old One or Ment but Agbar, his beloved personal slave who had also gone with the caravan. Agbar came directly up to the king and opened his arms just as the king had his arms also open wide.

"Why are you here?" the king asked in astonishment. "Why have you returned? Did I not grant you your freedom?"

"Even as a slave, oh king, you shared your life with me. You have given me freedom, but I have seen the true "King of Peace." And in true freedom I have returned to share with you this "King of Peace," and my God, the everlasting God of the Universe.

Beginning of the End

As you can see from these sketches of people who may have been there the night Jesus was born, each was affected in a different way. From the tearful misunderstanding of the father to the realization and anticipation of the old Rabbi, each one reacted in their own way to the birth in the stable.

So it is today when the birth of Jesus is brought into view. Some do not understand, some just ignore it as nothing, and some know it as the promise and the future of mankind and the entire world.

May we all, as the little shepherd boy, grow with a Holy desire to see Jesus, the Christ, knowing that if we turn away, we may never see him.

The Call

This book, even though fiction, is about a baby who is the true savior to everyone who confesses their sins and asks for forgiveness. The promise of God is for <u>all</u> without exception. If you would like to be part of the promise of eternity, below is the way.

THE PROBLEM
Romans 3:23 – All have sinned and fall short of the glory of God

THE CONSEQUENCE
Romans 6:23 – The wages of sin is death, but the free gift of God is eternal life in Jesus Christ, our Lord

THE SOLUTION, HE PAID OUR PENALTY
Romans 5:8 – While we were yet sinners, Jesus Christ died for us

THE RESPONSE

Romans 10:9-10 – If you confess with your mouth
that Jesus Christ is Lord,
And believe in your heart that God raised Him
from the dead, you will be saved

THE ASSURANCE

Romans 10:13 – Whoever will call on the
name of the Lord will be saved

(Above scripture references on this page
are from the New American Standard Bible)

About the Author

From the time Chuck learned to read, he read everything he could find. He also had a strong imagination, and with that imagination, constantly looked at himself as part of the stories he read. He began teaching and sharing his stories from the Bible at the age of seventeen in Sunday school classes, and has continued this path through college while earning two music degrees.

He has also served thirty years in the Army and National Guard. He and his wife Mary, from Lincoln, Nebraska, met in West Berlin, Germany, and settled in Lincoln Nebraska. They have two married sons, five grandchildren and four great grandchildren.

Chuck has continued his teaching by managing a campus for Christian Life International Bible College for over five years. He has sung in a Gospel Quartet for over thirty years, and has also served on a volunteer fire and rescue department for seventeen years.

He always comes back to the Bible for his stories and dreams. Chuck's current work in progress illuminates the life of a member of the Sanhedrin during the time of Jesus.

More from Charles G. Dorsey

GAMALIEL

What happens when you know the truth
and are helpless against the wrong?
Dorsey's next offering will bring to life
Gamaliel and his friends of the Sanhedrin
who are helpless in the trial of Jesus.

www.ingramcontent.com/pod-product-compliance
Lightning Source LLC
Chambersburg PA
CBHW060425260626
47161CB00005B/1783